"Where Am I Supposed To Sleep?"

Dakota patted the space next to him and grinned. "Right next to your husband, darlin', like a good little wife."

Annie blew an agitated breath. So Dakota had agreed to marry her and adopt the kids. That didn't mean she had to offer herself to him like a sacrificial lamb.

She stopped pacing and stared down at him. There he was, his arms resting behind his head, looking like the King of Siam in her bed. She narrowed her eyes. "I should have found another Cheyenne to marry."

He grinned back at her. "You don't know any other Cheyenne men. Now quit acting like a baby and get in bed. I don't bite."

No, but he could turn her insides to mush with a kiss. Annie breathed deeply for strength and stepped toward the bed. Thank goodness she was no longer a crush-crazed teenager, marveling at his virility. So what was that fluttering in her stomach...and in her heart?

Dear Reader,

Silhouette is celebrating its 20th anniversary throughout 2000! So, to usher in the first summer of the millennium, why not indulge yourself with six powerful, passionate, provocative love stories from Silhouette Desire?

Jackie Merritt returns to Desire with a MAN OF THE MONTH who's *Tough To Tame.* Enjoy the sparks that fly between a rugged ranch manager and the feisty lady who turns his world upside down! Another wonderful romance from RITA Award winner Caroline Cross is in store for you this month with *The Rancher and the Nanny,* in which a rags-to-riches hero learns trust and love from the riches-to-rags woman who cares for his secret child.

Watch for Meagan McKinney's *The Cowboy Meets His Match*—an octogenarian matchmaker sets up an ice-princess heiress with a virile rodeo star. The Desire theme promotion THE BABY BANK, about sperm-bank client heroines who find love unexpectedly, concludes with Susan Crosby's *The Baby Gift.* Wonderful newcomer Sheri WhiteFeather offers another irresistible Native American hero with *Cheyenne Dad.* And Kate Little's hero reunites with his lost love in a marriage of convenience to save her from financial ruin in *The Determined Groom.*

So come join in the celebration and start your summer off on the supersensual side—by reading all six of these tantalizing Desire books!

Enjoy!

Joan Marlow Golan

Joan Marlow Golan
Senior Editor, Silhouette Desire

Please address questions and book requests to:
Silhouette Reader Service
U.S.: 3010 Walden Ave., P.O. Box 1325, Buffalo, NY 14269
Canadian: P.O. Box 609, Fort Erie, Ont. L2A 5X3

Cheyenne Dad
SHERI WHITEFEATHER

Published by Silhouette Books

America's Publisher of Contemporary Romance

To Nikki WhiteFeather and his cousins:
Rachel McCafferty, Laicee Chandler, Miles McCullough,
Patrick and Parker Henry.
You are all great kids.

 SILHOUETTE BOOKS

ISBN 0-373-76300-X

CHEYENNE DAD

Copyright © 2000 by Sheree Henry-WhiteFeather

Visit Silhouette at www.eHarlequin.com

Printed in U.S.A.

Books by Sheri WhiteFeather

Silhouette Desire

Warrior's Baby #1248
Skyler Hawk: Lone Brave #1272
Jesse Hawk: Brave Father #1278
Cheyenne Dad #1300

SHERI WHITEFEATHER

lives in Southern California and enjoys ethnic dining, summer powwows and visiting art galleries and vintage clothing stores near the beach. Since her one true passion is writing, she is thrilled to be a part of the Silhouette Desire line. When she isn't writing, she often reads until the wee hours of the morning.

Sheri also works as a leather artisan with her Muscogee Creek husband. They have one son and a menagerie of pets, including a pampered English bulldog and four equally spoiled Bengal cats. She would love to hear from her readers. You may write to her at: P.O. Box 5130, Orange, California 92863-5130.

IT'S OUR 20th ANNIVERSARY!
We'll be celebrating all year,
Continuing with these fabulous titles,
On sale in June 2000.

Romance

#1450 Cinderella's Midnight Kiss
Dixie Browning

#1451 Promoted—To Wife!
Raye Morgan

AN OLDER MAN
#1452 Professor and the Nanny
Phyllis Halldorson

The Circle K Sisters
#1453 Never Let You Go
Judy Christenberry

The WEDDING AUCTION
#1454 Contractually His
Myrna Mackenzie

#1455 Just the Husband She Chose
Karen Rose Smith

Desire

MAN OF THE MONTH
#1297 Tough To Tame
Jackie Merritt

#1298 The Rancher and the Nanny
Caroline Cross

MATCHED IN MONTANA
#1299 The Cowboy Meets His Match
Meagan McKinney

#1300 Cheyenne Dad
Sheri WhiteFeather

 the Baby Bank
#1301 The Baby Gift
Susan Crosby

#1302 The Determined Groom
Kate Little

Intimate Moments

 The WILDES *of* WYOMING
#1009 The Wildes of Wyoming—Ace
Ruth Langan

 These Marrying McBrides!
#1010 The Best Man
Linda Turner

#1011 Beautiful Stranger
Ruth Wind

#1012 Her Secret Guardian
Sally Tyler Hayes

#1013 Undercover with the Enemy
Christine Michels

#1014 The Lawman's Last Stand
Vickie Taylor

Special Edition

#1327 The Baby Quilt
Christine Flynn

#1328 Irish Rebel
Nora Roberts

 Baby Boy
#1329 To a MacAllister Born
Joan Elliott Pickart

 A Family Bond
#1330 A Man Apart
Ginna Gray

DESERT ROGUES
#1331 The Sheik's Secret Bride
Susan Mallery

#1332 The Price of Honor
Janis Reams Hudson

One

How many days had she pleaded her case? Begged Harold to change his mind?

Annie Winters sat at her desk in the back room of her retail store, cradling the phone to her ear. "Please, be reasonable."

Harold's breath rasped through the receiver. The eighty-six-year-old Cheyenne lived on a reservation in Montana, nine hundred miles away from Annie's hometown in Southern California, yet he held her future in the flick of a ballpoint pen. She needed his signature. Desperately.

"My granddaughter was married," he stated stoically. "She had a husband."

Annie stared across the room, as an image of her dear friend came to mind. Jill with her shining black hair and crooked smile. Jill, the biological mother of the children Annie intended to adopt, the boys she had come to love with all her heart. Yes, Jill had been happily married to the father of her children until a car accident had taken both of their lives two years before, making orphans of their three young sons.

Annie sighed. "I don't have a man in my life, Harold. I can't just pull a husband out of a hat."

"I won't sign the adoption papers unless you get married. You can't be both parents no matter how hard you try. My great-grandchildren need a father."

Annie shifted the phone. After Jill's death she had altered her life-style, knowing the children needed her. She'd started a new business, bought a new home, grieved with the boys, cradled them, kissed their skinned knees and watched them grow.

How could Harold expect her to survive without gap-toothed grins and sweet, warm hugs? Youthful chatter and jelly-stained clothes? "You can't take them away from me. You just can't."

But he could, and they both knew it. Without Harold's consent she would lose the children. Harold was their only legal living relative. He had the power to grant the private adoption she had been pursuing.

She squeezed her eyes shut, dreading her fate. Harold wasn't insisting she marry just any man; he'd firmly stated that her future husband must be a registered Cheyenne, someone able to teach the children about that side of their heritage.

And there was only one man in her acquaintance who fitted that description.

Dakota Graywolf.

Drawing a deep breath, Annie opened her eyes. Dakota had scheduled a trip to see the boys. He'd be arriving within two weeks. That gave her fourteen days to muster the courage to propose to the last man on earth she wanted to marry.

Two weeks later, a single-lane highway led Annie to the Sleep Shack, a motel as tired and run-down as its name. The dilapidated pink structure sat on the outskirts of a dusty California town, blistering and peeling in the harsh desert sun.

Of the three trucks parked in the narrow lot, she recognized his immediately. He drove a bright-red pickup, an American-made model displaying generous mud flaps, squashed bugs on the windshield and wide tires with plenty of tread.

She exited her minivan and smoothed her blouse, straightening the embroidered collar. As she made her way to the motel door, the desert winds played havoc with her hair and billowed her ankle-length skirt, taunting yards of blue silk.

Annie knocked, and Dakota Graywolf flung open the door and stared down at her from his towering height. His black eyes sparked beneath even blacker brows before he offered a familiar greeting.

"Hey, squirt."

She cringed at the nickname he wouldn't allow her to outgrow, then tried to summon a smile. Dakota used to tease her unmercifully when they were kids, knowing full well she'd had a painful crush on him. And by the time they were both adults, he'd taken that crush and used it against her, smiling that rakish smile, undressing her with those ebony eyes. Of course, it was all a game, part of his flirtatious nature. Women, she surmised, were a form of entertainment to Dakota Graywolf.

Annie lifted her chin. He wasn't exactly white-picket-fence material, but she didn't have a choice. "Thanks for agreeing to see me."

"Sure. Come on in."

He stepped away from the door, and she walked into his seedy motel room, struggling to keep her nerves in check.

The unmade bed and Dakota's rangy form were both slightly tousled. Thick black hair teased his nape and fell rebelliously across his forehead. A pair of cowboy-cut jeans hugged his hips, the top snap undone, exposing the elastic waistband of his briefs. His bronze-toned chest, slightly scarred and generously muscled, made her all too aware of their gender difference.

Annie glanced back at the bed again and couldn't help but wonder if he'd shared it with someone the previous night. If anyone was capable of finding a lover in the middle of nowhere, it was Dakota Graywolf. He collected beautiful women the way fleece garments collected lint.

Should she care? No, but the nature of her visit explained why she did.

"Have a seat." Dakota offered her a cold soda and pointed to the Formica table positioned by the window.

She settled into one of the wobbly chairs and watched him move toward the other one. Although he limped a little, she marveled at his determination. Two years before, Dakota had suffered a rodeo injury that could have left him paralyzed, had he not had the will to walk again. Too many tragedies had occurred that year. Dakota had been trampled by a bull in the same month that Jill and her husband had died.

Annie studied him, wishing her stomach would settle. He looked well. Better than well, but she decided to keep the compliment to herself. She knew he didn't like to talk about the accident or discuss the details of his recovery. And since he had been in Montana rehabilitating from his injuries, and she lived in California, they hadn't seen each other in over two years.

What a reunion, she thought, twisting her hands on her lap.

Would he accept her proposal? Surely he, of all people, would understand. Jill had been like a sister to him. He wouldn't turn his back on her children. He was their "Uncle Kody," the famous cowboy, the World Champion Bull Rider who called regularly and sent bushels of toys.

He reached for the cigarette pack on the table, slipped one out, then flicked open a sterling lighter. The cigarette bobbed as a half smile curved one corner of his lips. "So here we are, squirt."

"Yes, here we are." In a seedy motel room. Together. His jeans unsnapped and her skin as warm as the desert air.

Annie opened the soda, eager to taste the cool liquid. Once again, her gaze strayed to the bed. She should have asked him to meet her at a coffee shop, someplace bright and busy. Impersonal. Suddenly she didn't feel as though she'd known this man for eighteen years or that they'd kept in touch by phone for the past two. Dakota seemed like a stranger, not the self-imposed uncle of the children she intended to adopt. He was, at the moment, a half-naked man in a dimly lit motel room.

He followed her glance, to the rumpled sheets. "Hey I know this place is a dive, but I just drove halfway across the country. When you're on the road, any bed will do."

True, but he hadn't slept in just any bed, she thought. He'd slept in the one only a few feet away, the imprint of his head still on the pillow.

Annie cursed that unmade bed and the man who had slept in

it. Dakota never seemed to mind the heat that sizzled between them, but she did. She'd gotten tangled up with his type before, a man she thought she could tame. Maybe her ex-fiancé wasn't a reckless cowboy, but he'd been a womanizer just the same.

And then there was her father, the handsome rake who'd charmed her mother as often as he'd cheated on her. Annie's dad had been a bull rider, just like Dakota. Only he hadn't survived his career.

Annie hated the rodeo and everything it represented. Guilt gnawed at her whenever she thought about her father. Even as a child, she'd understood why her mother had divorced Clay Winters. Her dad had overindulged in the fringe benefits of being a professional cowboy, getting drunk in honky-tonk bars and sleeping with easy women. It had hurt to love a man who had disrespected his family so blatantly. But it also hurt to think about that bull puncturing his lung, stealing his youth and vitality.

"What's going on?" Dakota asked, drawing her attention back to him. "Why did you drive clear out here instead of waiting for me to come to your house? I was on my way to see the boys."

The boys. Her babies. She had to talk to Dakota without the children present. She didn't want them to know she'd been railroaded into making this decision. She tried to keep a sense of normalcy in their lives, and this situation was anything but normal.

"When's the last time you saw Harold?" she asked. "Did you visit with him before you left Montana?"

"Yeah, I saw him. He sends his love."

"He didn't say anything else? You know, about me adopting the kids?"

"Of course he mentioned the kids, but he didn't say anything about the adoption." Dakota drew on the cigarette, then blew a stream of smoke to the ceiling. "But then that's between you and him."

Not anymore, Annie thought. Dakota had just been tossed into the mix. "Harold won't give me legal custody unless I get married," she began, watching Dakota's startled expression.

"He wants the boys to be raised in a traditional setting, with a mother and a father."

He leaned into the table. "You're joking, right? An arranged marriage? That sounds like something from the Dark Ages."

Annie swallowed another sip of the drink. "There's more to it than that. Harold expects me to marry a Cheyenne, someone who can teach the boys about their heritage." She wrapped her fingers around the can, held it tight. "And that's when I thought of you. You're already like an uncle to the kids, and in your culture, an uncle is practically a second father."

Rather than respond, Dakota studied her through those dark, indiscernible eyes. She felt his gaze on her face, her hands, her nervous fingers as they gripped the soda. Once again she became aware of the tousled bed, the dimness of the room, the breadth of his shoulders. Now she wanted to throttle him for answering the door half-naked. A gentleman would have slipped on a shirt and fastened his jeans.

"Damn it, Dakota, say something."

A column of dusky gray ashes gathered on the end of his cigarette. He squinted through the haze of smoke, then flicked the ashes, nearly missing his mark. "Are you asking me to marry you?"

Annie lifted her chin, feigning a sense of bravado she didn't quite feel. This was, by far, the most humiliating experience of her life. "I'm asking for the sake of the kids."

He stared at her again, another long, thoughtful stare. Annie exhaled a shaky breath. Was he going to refuse? Say, Sorry, you've got the wrong guy. I like my freedom. A wife will cramp my style. Marrying you is going above and beyond the call of duty.

All she was asking for was a marriage of convenience. She would never expect a man like Dakota to be a real husband. Besides, that wasn't what she wanted, either. What she wanted, Annie decided, was to turn and walk away. Yet she couldn't. She had three little boys depending on her. And those children were far more important than her pride.

Dakota stamped out his cigarette, then dragged a hand through his hair. The unsettling look in Annie's whisky-colored eyes told him plenty. She was worried he would brush her off with without a second thought.

Well, she was wrong. He intended to accept her proposal. But then why wouldn't he? He'd known it was coming long before Annie did. He'd known for two years.

Dakota had agreed to be Jill's blood brother when they were kids, vowing to honor and protect her—a Cheyenne vow that later included her children, as well. So with that in mind, he hadn't been surprised when Harold had approached him about adopting Jill's orphaned boys. The shock had come when Harold had proclaimed, "It's your duty to marry Annie and give the children a proper home."

"Mar-r-y Annie?" Dakota had stuttered.

"You want to bed her," Harold had responded in that stoic manner of his.

Dakota had raised an eyebrow at that, an emotional ache poisoning his gut like a snakebite. It was true, he'd been lusting after Annie for over a decade, fantasizing like a randy schoolboy over the pert little blonde. But he couldn't bed anyone. His legs didn't work, and neither did the body part he'd always taken for granted. His crippling injury had left him impotent.

"I'll adopt the kids, but I won't marry Annie."

"It's your place to do so," Harold insisted, invoking his status as Dakota's elder. "Annie needs a husband as much as the boys need a father. I won't allow her to raise those children by herself. If you refuse to marry her, I'll find someone who will."

Dakota stared at his lap, cursing the legs that wouldn't move. How could Harold expect him to become Annie's husband?

Because, he told himself several days later, he was supposed to be a warrior. A fighter. A man who had no right to turn his back on a woman and three children, no matter how much the idea of marriage scared him.

Dakota's life had been spared in that accident, so maybe now Maheo, the Creator, was asking him to give something back. Duty and honor were a part of his heritage he had neglected for far too long.

"If it's my place, I'll marry her," he announced, "but not

until I can walk again." *And make love,* he added mentally, deciding then and there that he'd be the best damn lover Annie Winters had ever had. All he needed was time. Determination. And plenty of prayer.

So Harold had agreed to keep the arranged nuptials a secret from Annie until Dakota regained the use of his legs. Only Dakota had taken it a step further. "She has to do the asking," he'd told the older man. "Marrying me has to be her idea."

Dakota studied Annie's anxious expression. No, he couldn't tell her the truth. She didn't need to know that he had battled his injury so he could play ball with the kids, race through a meadow on horseback, ease himself into her arms on their wedding night.

He swiped his drink and took a huge swallow. He would never reveal that he had been preparing himself to become a husband and father—a family man.

Yeah, right. He scowled and placed the soda back on the table. Dakota Graywolf was, and probably always would be, a troubled cowboy. A rodeo champion who'd been trampled by the orneriest, most infamous bull in existence—a wreck that had inflicted more than just a physical challenge. Dakota had been plagued with anxiety ever since the accident, reliving the fall, over and over in his mind. The only cure, he knew, was getting back on that bull. And he would someday, but for now he had another priority.

"So you're looking for a husband, huh?" he asked, faking nonchalance.

"Because of the children," she reiterated.

"When would I have to do this?"

She gripped her soda can a little tighter. "As soon as possible. Are you saying yes?"

He wondered if he should hedge, drag out his answer. If he seemed too eager, she might figure out that he'd been forewarned. "I don't know, I mean…" He watched her eyes cloud with fear and felt a lump of guilt form in his throat.

"Sure, I'll do it. You know, for the kids. I am their uncle, and you're right, in my culture that pretty much makes me their father already. And marrying you won't be that bad," he added for effect. "Hell, we've known each other for over half of our lives."

She reached for his hand, touched it lightly. "Thank you. I'm sure Harold will approve. I've been so worried about losing the boys, but now…"

Although Annie's voice quavered, her smile radiated genuine warmth, sending heat flaring through Dakota's veins. He gazed at her lips, the rosy color and soft texture. She was beautiful. Dangerously beautiful. A feisty kid who had blossomed into an incredible woman.

"We need to make arrangements," she said.

He studied the length of her hair, the pale color. With her white-blond hair and amber eyes, she reminded him of a lioness, a naturally sexy creature. And she owned a lingerie store, which had him constantly wondering what sort of lacy little underthings she wore. "I'm sorry. What did you say?"

"We need to set a wedding date, so I can tell Harold. I want to make sure he gets the adoption proceedings started."

A lioness protecting her cubs, Dakota decided. "Yeah, okay. How about Las Vegas? Weddings are quick and easy there. I know Vegas pretty well." The National Finals Rodeo was held in Las Vegas every year. He knew that town better than well.

"That's fine. We should get this done as simply as possible. And I should probably get a sitter for the kids, too. Traveling would only wear them out." She brushed a lock of hair from her eye. "Besides, it's not as if this is going to be a real marriage. There's no reason to make a fuss over the ceremony."

He cocked his head. "Weddings in Vegas are real, Annie. They're legal."

She reached for her drink. "I know. But ours will be just a business deal. No love. No sex. That's hardly a real marriage."

Dakota's heart nearly stopped.

No sex?

"You can't be serious."

The stern look she shot him said otherwise. She was serious, all right. She had no intention of sleeping with him.

Dakota righted his posture as a hot fist of anger clenched his gut. Anger to mask the pain, he thought. The disappointment. The horrible rejection.

Did she have any idea how long he had struggled to regain the use of his body? Two years. Twenty-four months of promising himself Annie Winters would be his reward at the end of long, grueling road. She was supposed to become his lover, the woman he would stroke and caress, hold on to at night.

"Fine, Annie. Whatever." He wasn't about to beg for his conjugal rights. He'd suffered enough humiliation.

She breathed what sounded like a sigh of relief, and he cursed what he was about to become—a man with a gorgeous wife and a nonexistent love life.

As Annie watched Dakota walk across the airport terminal, the butterflies in her stomach fluttered. He moved like a cowboy—long, lean and just a little bit mean. With a duffel bag slung over his arm, a Stetson dipped over his eyes and Wranglers hugging him like a well-worn glove, he drew plenty of attention. Somehow the slight limp rather added to his don't-mess-with-me charm.

"There he is." Mary Graywolf leaned forward. "Hmm. He doesn't look too happy, does he?"

Annie tilted her head. He looked about as ornery as the bulls he used to ride. She had the feeling Dakota wasn't particularly pleased about the no-sex clause in their marriage, but she knew their union would end once the adoption was finalized. Although grateful for his loyalty to the children, she wasn't about to allow Dakota Graywolf to have some fun with her, then toss her aside.

"You know how moody your big brother can be."

"No kidding. Just look at that macho attitude."

Mary rolled her eyes, and Annie nibbled on a smile. She adored Mary. Her dear friend, Annie had decided long ago, was the only good that had come out of her father's short-lived career.

Annie's dad and Mary's dad had been rodeo buddies, often traveling the same circuit, a teenage Dakota in tow. So consequently, after Annie's dad had died, she'd spent youthful summers in Montana with the Graywolf family. The Graywolfs, it seemed, had influenced her life for nearly two decades now. It was through them that she had also met Jill.

Annie turned her attention back to Dakota. He strode toward them, dropped his bag onto the chair beside Mary, then glared down at his sister. She stood and glared back at him. The siblings looked like gunslingers preparing to draw.

He fired first. "What are you, the chaperone?"

She flipped the brim of his hat. "That's right. I'm here to make sure you behave yourself."

"Great." He slipped the hat back down. "Just what I need. My bossy sister along on what's supposed to be my honeymoon."

Ignoring both women, Dakota slumped onto a chair and crossed his arms over his chest, long legs stretched out before him.

Mary sat down as well. "They'll probably let us board soon."

"Wonderful." Dakota didn't try to mask the sarcasm in his tone.

Annie leaned over. "Hello, Kody," she said, using the nickname the boys had given him. She wasn't about to let his sour attitude intimidate her. They certainly couldn't snarl at each other in front of the children, so they may as well learn to be polite now. "It's nice to see you."

He reached into his front pocket for a cigarette. The Western shirt boasted whipcord trim and a pearl-snap placket. "Yeah, squirt. Likewise."

Annie studied his brooding posture. How tall was the man who still insisted on calling her squirt? Well over six feet. Of course, the black hat and scuffed leather boots intensified his threatening demeanor. Even seated, he looked rough and rangy.

"It's a nonsmoking flight," Mary said when Dakota lit up.

He scowled. "Do we look like we're on the plane yet?"

Annie noticed he inhaled as though savoring each drag, a reminder that she would have to enforce the No Smoking rule at home. She insisted on a healthy environment for the kids. Dakota would just have to smoke outside.

He stamped out his cigarette when their flight number was called. As he stood, a huddle of attractive young women craned their necks. For some odd reason Annie wanted to scratch their eyes out. Sex or no sex, he'd still be her husband.

Temporary husband, she amended, calming herself. Six months, tops. Annie chewed her bottom lip, then glanced at Dakota. It wasn't as though she was purposely deceiving Harold. The children would always have Dakota as a father. But common sense told her the adoption would outlive the marriage. Free-spirited men, much like leopards, didn't change their spots. Dakota Graywolf would be pining for his freedom in no time.

They shuffled into a line and waited for the passengers who either required assistance or were traveling with small children to board first.

After a frazzled woman boarded with her active toddler, Dakota turned to Annie. "You know, I was thinking that there's no need for you to take the kids to a baby-sitter this summer. I can watch them."

Disbelief widened her eyes. "But what about your work? Don't you have orders to fill?" Since Dakota had retired from the rodeo, he'd turned his silversmith hobby into a business. She knew he planned to set up a workshop in her garage.

He adjusted the duffel bag. "Sure, but how much trouble can three little rug rats be?"

Annie caught Mary's raised eyebrow and they both erupted into one of their giggling fits. The "rug rats," ages two, five and eight, each had their own special personality. Besides being adorable—*possessive, serious* and *rambunctious* described them to a T.

"What's so funny?" he asked between clenched teeth.

"You." Mary bumped his shoulder with a sisterly shove. A psychology major with a minor in theater arts, Mary analyzed everyone and offered advice without being asked. "You have no idea what supervising small children is like. You haven't seen the boys in two years. Maybe you should consider easing into fatherhood."

"I call the kids all the time," Dakota argued. "Every week."

Mary continued to chuckle. "That doesn't mean they're going to behave while you work."

He dismissed her opinion with the wave of his hand. "Yeah? Just wait and see." He cocked his head toward Annie. "You, too, squirt."

Annie ceased her laughter. How many times a day must that annoying nickname surface?

They boarded the plane and sat three across. Dakota ended up in the middle because Mary wanted to look out the window and Annie preferred the aisle.

When they were airborne, a female flight attendant came down the aisle offering a drink and two bags of peanuts. Annie and Mary both ordered a soft drink.

Dakota readjusted his long limbs for the third time. "Give me one of those little bottles of—" he glanced over at Annie and their eyes met "—whisky."

Uncomfortable, Annie looked away. He used to say a man could get drunk on her whisky-colored eyes. Was he trying to make that flirtatious point now, or did he usually drink his breakfast?

After the attendant moved on, Dakota turned to his sister. "Don't you dare say a word."

"Sure." She popped a peanut into her mouth. "Everybody knows 10:00 a.m. is the perfect cocktail hour."

When the whisky arrived, he apologized for the inconvenience and asked if he could have a glass of water instead. "I changed my mind," he said, staring into Annie's eyes once again.

As his dark gaze moved down her body, she crossed her legs, then uncrossed them, glad the fold-out tray concealed most of her. She had chosen to travel in an almond-colored cotton pantsuit accented with a suede belt and sling-back heels. Annie had a professional yet stylish wardrobe; she had graduated from college with a degree in fashion design.

As Dakota's gaze seared his approval, she swallowed the lump in her throat. She almost felt as though he were mentally undressing her. Almost. He glanced away before she could be sure. Maybe he got as far as popping open a few buttons, she decided, actually checking the front of her blouse to be sure they were in place.

As her hand crept to her second button, his lips twitched. The fleeting smile had a sensuality attached that made her cheeks feel flushed.

"What's the matter?" he asked.

Annie stopped fidgeting with her buttons. "Nothing."

The twitching smile returned. "Guess what, squirt? I booked us the honeymoon suite."

Annie glanced over at Mary, hoping she might intervene, but the other woman wore headphones and was tapping in time to the music selection she had chosen.

"*Dakota.*"

Amusement danced in his black eyes. "What?"

Suddenly she wished he'd go back to his brooding self. "I'm sharing a room with Mary."

"Yeah, I know. I was just kidding around." He tore open one of the little peanut bags. "But haven't you ever wondered about honeymoon suites? Like do they have mirrors above the beds or heart-shaped hot tubs or what?"

Actually she had but wouldn't dare admit it. "It never crossed my mind." Images of being with Dakota Graywolf in a honeymoon suite could prove dangerous.

He shifted his legs for what had to be the fourth or fifth time. Definitely too tall for coach, she decided. "Six-one," she said, thinking out loud.

He answered what he must have thought was a question. "Two. Three in boots. And I hate these coach flights."

Annie couldn't resist a smirk. "This suits me just fine. I'm still a squirt." Teasing about the childhood nickname seemed easier than complaining about it. Besides, maybe it was safer having him regard her as "squirt" rather than a woman.

He finished off the peanuts and stuffed the bag into his empty water cup. "Yeah, you're still little, but you grew up beautiful. Just like I knew you would."

Annie turned toward the aisle as the flight attendant neared, grateful for the interruption. Dakota's hushed tone and gentle words had sounded like a bedroom whisper. Intimate and husky.

The attendant took their empty cups and moved on just as the plane hit a pocket of turbulence.

Several passengers murmured, and more than one pair of eyes popped open as the plane bumped and jarred. Annie, an inexperienced flyer, gripped her armrest for support, unintentionally catching Dakota's hand.

His fingers curled around hers. "You okay?"

"I don't like being away from the kids." She let him hold her hand because the gesture made her feel safe. He had protective hands, large and slightly callused. "If something happened to us…"

He rubbed his fingertips over her knuckles. "Nothing's going to happen. It's just a little turbulence."

"I know. It's the first time I've spent a night away."

As the plane steadied and the other anxious passengers relaxed, Annie's gaze locked with Dakota's, and an awkward silence stretched between them. Although their fingers were still entwined, neither attempted to break the connection.

Annie watched his chest rise and fall, wondering if the contact had made his heart beat as erratically as hers. Not likely, she thought. Things like rapid heartbeats and stomach butterflies didn't happen to men. Not men like him, anyway.

She slid her hand away and immediately folded up the tray and latched it, telling herself that her reaction had been perfectly normal. Just airplane jitters. She hadn't been electrocuted by six foot plus of beautifully sculpted male. Tall and sinfully handsome didn't affect her anymore. Her ex-fiancé had curbed that craving long ago.

Mary popped her headphones off and grinned. "That was fun, wasn't it? That roller-coaster action."

"Yeah." Dakota clasped his hands in front of him as though ensuring they wouldn't collide with Annie's again. "We're having a blast, aren't we, darlin'?"

"Oh, sure." Annie nodded, hoping she appeared calmer than she felt. Her heart had yet to resume its steady rhythm.

Two

Annie sat beside Mary on a gold-flecked bench in the tiny waiting room of the chapel, gazing at the decor. "This place is—"

"Gaudy," the other woman provided with a smirk.

Annie nodded. *Gaudy* fit. Everything, including the textured wallpaper, had been gold-leafed. The design on the maroon-and-royal-blue carpet clashed with the green drapes, the kind, Annie mused, Scarlett O'Hara had fashioned a dress from. In her opinion, Scarlett's imaginative dress certainly looked better than the windows here did. She gazed around again and winced, then widened her eyes when Dakota entered the room, carrying a bouquet of white roses and a yellow corsage. He slipped the corsage onto his sister's wrist and handed Annie the roses.

"They sell flowers here," he said by way of explanation, his shoulders rising with a slight shrug.

Pleasantly surprised by the thoughtful gesture, Annie thanked him, while Mary reacted like a dutiful sister and stood to fuss with his hair. As Mary brushed a stray lock from Dakota's eye, Annie hugged the delicate bouquet to her chest and studied him. Not only had the groom provided flowers, he'd worn a suit, one that appeared tailor-made for his wide shoulders and slim hips. The black jacket intensified the depth of his eyes as a white Western shirt, adorned with chain-stitch embroidery and tiny glass beads, emphasized the copper glow of his skin. In lieu of a tie he wore an engraved silver bolo.

As Mary attempted to right Dakota's hair, Annie noticed it appeared to have a mind of its own. When the tousled chunk his sister had meticulously finger combed came falling back onto his forehead, she couldn't help but smile. Annie liked the way his hair rebelled, thinking it fit his renegade style. Even impeccably dressed, Dakota Graywolf had an untamed quality.

Eventually Mary gave up on her brother's hair, choosing to peck his cheek with a quick kiss instead. Much to Annie's amazement, Dakota responded favorably to his sister's affection, returning her kiss with a hug. Apparently the rough-and-tumble cowboy hadn't outgrown the need to be mothered.

Mary spoke quietly to her brother, then turned to Annie. She looked pretty, her black hair flowing like a river of silk and her strong features softened by an artful hint of makeup. The yellow corsage matched the flowers sprinkled on her chiffon dress, reminding Annie of prom night rather than a tacky Las Vegas wedding.

"I'll be back in a minute," Mary said. "I need to powder my nose."

"Okay." As the other woman headed in the direction of the ladies' room, Annie chose not to follow. She'd powdered her own nose quite enough. She'd labored over her appearance far longer than necessary, especially considering the circumstances surrounding this wedding.

Besides, if she wanted to peer at her carefully coifed image, all she had to do was gaze into the gilded mirror that, at the moment, reflected the back of Dakota's head and the thick black mass brushing his collar.

Why were men always graced with the longest eyelashes and most luxuriant hair? An impressive gene pool had certainly

given Dakota both. And more. Unfortunately, even his imper-
fections, like a crooked eyebrow interrupted by a narrow scar,
managed to bewitch her.

Dakota tapped a booted foot while Annie nibbled her bottom
lip and watched his patience wear thin. The wedding prior to
theirs had gotten a late start.

"Shouldn't be much longer," she said.

He stopped tapping and looked down at her, dark eyes rov-
ing. With an impassive gaze, he examined her from the top of
her loosely styled hair to the tips of her satin pumps. She knew
what he eyed in between was white silk embellished by a
strand of pearls. Annie had chosen a simple yet elegant dress
for her unconventional wedding. The timeless style comple-
mented her figure without flaunting the abundant curves she
often struggled to conceal. In her opinion, fashionable women
should appear lithe with long graceful lines, not top-heavy with
hips better suited to a fifties pinup.

Dakota sat beside her, and Annie glanced down at the simple bouquet on her lap, recalling the lavish details of what had
almost been her first wedding: the carefully chosen china pat-
terns, the gilded invitations, the Victorian-style gown she'd
burned just hours after she'd caught Richard in bed with Sheila
Harris.

Three days before their wedding date, she'd stumbled upon
her fiancé, her college sweetheart, in bed with a former lover.
Richard, a gifted quarterback, had been a popular man on cam-
pus with his California tan and easy smile.

Annie had been young and naive where Richard was concerned, believing she could change him. She'd known about
his wild flirtations but was certain "the right woman" would
make a difference. Annie had fallen into an age-old trap—the
good girl hell-bent on redeeming the handsome bad boy.

A good girl. A virgin. That was her, all right. Since she had
saved herself for a traditional wedding night, she'd convinced
Richard to wait until they were married to consummate their
union. And after that devastating relationship had faltered,
she'd spent the following years nit-picking anyone who could

have been a potential partner. Till this day, she still hadn't come across a man worth giving herself to.

Annie sighed. Richard had apologized profusely after she'd caught him cheating with his old flame, claiming it had happened in a "moment of weakness."

Yeah, right. It seemed every man she knew had experienced a weak moment or two with Sheila Harris. Including Dakota.

"Annie, where'd you go?"

Rather than turn to the sound of Dakota's voice, Annie continued to stare at the roses on her lap. "What?"

"You were zoning out." He drummed his fingers against his chair. "I guess you were thinking about *him*, huh?"

"Him?"

"That Joe-college jock you were engaged to."

Annie flinched, hating that Dakota had tapped into her thoughts. Why, damn it, couldn't she just forget all the pain associated with her last wedding? The gut-wrenching ache of betrayal? "You know darn well his name was Richard. And I wasn't thinking about him. I was just wondering what's taking them so long to get to us."

"Liar."

True, she thought. She had lied. And if there was anything she despised it was lies, betrayals, half-truths. "Being here like this reminds me of what happened," she said, struggling to steady her voice.

When Annie glanced up, Dakota trapped her gaze. Like polished onyx, his eyes reflected the light spilling from the chandelier. A man had no right being that striking, she thought, that physically appealing. Especially a man like Dakota.

"I'm sorry," he whispered.

Annie looked away. Was he apologizing for his involvement with Richard's old girlfriend? For that awful night both he and Richard had made her cry?

Dakota and Richard had met for the first time at Jill's twenty-first birthday party. And as Annie recalled, they'd despised each other on sight. From the moment she had introduced them, tension filled the air. Anyone within breathing distance could feel their testosterone levels rising. And to make matters worse, they had nearly come to blows over Sheila Harris—the sultry coed who had crashed the party just so she could keep an eye on Richard. The very woman who had ultimately worked her way back into his bed. After she'd tumbled into one with Dakota.

Annie and Richard had quarreled that evening. She had been angry that her boyfriend cared about who his ex-lover had attached herself to, and Richard had insisted that Dakota had hit on Sheila just to taunt him. Sheila, on the other hand, had behaved accordingly. She'd clung to Dakota like a curvaceous vine, flaunting her handsome catch.

Annie had cried herself to sleep that night, believing both Richard and Dakota should have respected her enough to avoid a public scene over Sheila Harris. Of course, like a naive little fool, she'd forgiven Richard just days later, when he'd presented her with a diamond ring and a proposal of forever.

Annie glanced at Dakota. How could this be happening? How could she be minutes away from marrying a man just like Richard?

She took a deep breath and told herself to relax. She wasn't in love with Dakota, nor had she promised to keep herself pure for him. The wedding night of her dreams wasn't going to happen with Dakota Graywolf. This was only a marriage of convenience—a business arrangement.

She gazed around the gaudy room, then closed her eyes. And it couldn't possibly last.

The small wedding party gathered at the back of the chapel as The Reverend Matthews, a white-haired man cloaked in a jeweled robe, took them through a brief narration of the ceremony. Although Dakota's concentration wavered, he caught what he considered the gist of it. Bea, the minister's equally tinseled wife, would provide the music, while Dakota stood at the flamboyant altar and waited for Annie to walk down the lavishly carpeted aisle. Mary would be there, as well, serving as witness and bridal attendant.

When the minister lifted his satin-draped arm and explained

at what point the rings would be exchanged, Annie piped up. "We don't have any."

"I do." Dakota reached into his pocket and produced a white-gold band set with a marquee-cut diamond and an intricate inlay of semi-precious stones.

Annie studied the ring glinting against his hand. "Is it one of yours?"

He nodded. He'd designed it for her for this day, but he couldn't tell her that. He doubted she'd be pleased about the secret he and Harold had been keeping. But then Dakota wasn't about to reveal the role she'd played in his recovery. He would rather die than suffer the mortification of her knowing the truth. Overcoming his paralysis and the impotency that had accompanied it wasn't something he could discuss with Annie. The loss of his virility, no matter how temporary, had made him feel like less of a man.

Annie leaned in close, drawing his attention back to the ring. "It's beautiful," she whispered, "but you didn't have to give me something so extravagant. I didn't expect a ring at all."

Her floral scent drifted to his nostrils, reminding him of how long he'd been waiting to bury his face in the fragrance of her hair.

Dakota shrugged and made a fist, pressing the diamond into his palm. "It's no big deal."

It was, of course. It hurt that she didn't want to make love with him. And now he couldn't help but wish that he'd kept his mouth shut about her other wedding. Richard had cheated on Annie with the same woman that Dakota had been with only months before. Mary had told him how upset Annie had been over that ordeal, how she'd felt as though Dakota had betrayed their friendship by "getting involved with Richard's old girlfriend."

Dakota shook his head. His "involvement" had been one stupid night that he'd regretted every day since.

Sheila had been a brazen one. Wearing a skimpy red dress designed to make a man drool, she'd sashayed up to him at that party and tossed her head, spilling golden waves around her shoulders. His immediate thought had been that she'd looked like a harder version of Annie. Blond and luscious, only lacking the inborn grace. But that hadn't mattered at the time, especially since Annie had been milling around the party with her Joe-college boyfriend.

Sheila made her first move by pressing her hand to Dakota's forehead. "You're hot for Richard's little girlfriend, aren't you? Burning right up with a fever."

Dakota's knees nearly buckled. No one had ever challenged him about his sexual attraction to Annie, the all-consuming ache he couldn't seem to shake. "Yeah, right. I've known her since she was a kid."

"Well, she's hardly a kid now," the blonde purred. "And you get excited just watching her breathe."

Dakota jerked away. "What the hell do you want?"

Sheila's painted lips curled into a naughty smile. "To make you forget all about her."

He should have walked away then. Game playing wasn't his style, but he wanted nothing more than to get Annie out of his system. Destroy the heat that surged through his blood every time he laid eyes on her.

The night had gone from bad to worse with Richard getting in his face, hissing words that were much too true. "What's the matter?" the jock had snarled in a quiet, menacing voice, "Are you stuck with my leftovers because you can't get the real thing?"

Blinded by rage, Dakota had lunged at the other man, knocking him against a wall. Richard had the woman he wanted, and there didn't seem to be a damn thing he could do about it. Nothing but take Sheila up on her offer. An offer that had made him sick and remorseful the following morning.

Swapping Sheila for Annie hadn't worked. And in the process he'd humiliated Annie and disgusted Mary and Jill, the women he cared most about.

"Looks to me like you folks are ready." The minister's voice boomed in Dakota's ear, jarring him from his disturbing thoughts.

Ready. Right. To marry a woman who had no intention of making love with him, of forgiving him for his sins. Annie had to suspect how many Sheila Harrises had slithered in and out of his bed. But that was his past, Dakota thought, the type of man he was before the accident.

"Sure," he said, faking a smile. "We're ready."

They took their places quietly, and when Bea began to plunk out a wedding march, brother and sister both turned to view the bride. As her hourglass figure swayed, Dakota's blood tingled. Annie Winters looked like a goddess: white-blond hair, a flowing white dress and a bouquet of white roses. As unique and pure, he decided, as a freshly fallen snowflake.

She stood beside him and stared straight ahead as the organ music ended and The Reverend Matthews began to speak. Dakota focused on Annie, on the way the sunlight streamed through the windows, highlighting her hair and illuminating her skin with a warm glow. The moment she repeated her vows and her gaze met his, his chest constricted. Her voice was soft and barely audible, but the words sounded sincere, as though they should have been spoken for another man, one she wanted to marry.

Dakota said his vows in the same near whisper, then removed the white-gold band from his pocket. The ring slid easily onto her finger.

"I pronounce you husband and wife," The Reverend Matthews said in a clear, strong voice, then smiled at Dakota. "Mr. Graywolf, you may kiss your bride."

Dakota turned toward Annie, and their eyes met. She looked sweet, he thought. Warm and girlish, yet womanly. He leaned in close and swallowed. "I'm supposed to do this," he whispered, praying she wouldn't flinch at his touch.

He skimmed his fingers down her back. Her whisky eyes grew doelike, but she didn't pull away, so he caressed her skin through the silk.

He encountered the outline of her undergarment, a wisp of lace beneath her dress. Closing his eyes, he brought his mouth to hers, then felt an immediate shiver rock them both.

Her lips yielded beneath his, just enough to send red-tipped sparks along his skin. Did she feel them, too? he wondered. The tiny, burning flames?

Annie placed her hands on Dakota's shoulders, intending to steady herself, but as her fingers crept forward, she caught a lock of his hair. That midnight hair. Thick and rebellious.

Without a second thought she parted her lips and allowed her husband access. Their tongues met in a desperate embrace, like strangers clinging to each other in a storm. No, she thought, a hurricane. A hurricane of desire. And loneliness, at least for her. It had been so long since she'd allowed a man to hold her close.

When the kiss ended, they stared at each other—an intimate gaze that defied all logic, all common sense. She watched him take a breath and felt her own hitch shakily. He towered over her, yet somehow their bodies seemed to fit. Still locked in an embrace, his pelvis brushed her stomach in a sensual tease, his chest a wall of iron against her breasts. Her nipples were hard, she realized. Hard and aching.

He dipped his head again, and she whispered his name and inhaled the faint spice of his cologne. It blended with a hint of leather and a pinch of tobacco, making him smell the way she imagined a reckless cowboy was supposed to smell. Earthy, masculine and forbidden.

He tasted forbidden, too. Heady, like a man who sipped brandy while he made love—satisfying a woman with slow, intoxicating strokes. Annie could almost imagine the naked feel of him, the virile mass of muscle and sinew beneath satin sheets. She moved closer and deepened the kiss, brushing herself against him. He groaned and licked her bottom lip, sucking it into his mouth.

Annie dived into a dream…a fantasy…a hotel room for lovers. If they shared a honeymoon suite tonight, they could soak in a heart-shaped tub, he could shampoo her hair, she could lather his….

"Oh, my goodness, they're going to eat each other alive."

Bea's shocked words broke the spell. Annie's heart jumped to her throat before she gave Dakota a quick, forceful shove. He staggered, frowned, then looked as embarrassed as she felt.

The minister, Bea and Mary all stood together, each with vivid expressions. Bea's mouth was agape, the minister wore a tight lip even though a smile danced in his eyes, and Mary, her dear friend, grinned like a hyena.

"That's it, then?" Dakota asked gruffly. "We're married?"

The Reverend Matthews nodded and extended his hand. "Yes. Congratulations."

The men shook hands and the minister bumped his wife's shoulder. "Oh, yes, congratulations," she squeaked.

Mary embraced Annie. "Now the kids will be legally yours." She chuckled. "You know, come to think of it, my brother is legally yours, too."

Annie sent the other woman a weak smile. Legally maybe, but not emotionally. Her honeymoon fantasy was just that. A fantasy. One she would never act upon. Once the adoption was final, this marriage would undoubtedly end. Dakota Graywolf was much too wild to remain married, and she was much too smart to expect otherwise.

She caught her bottom lip between her teeth. No matter how luscious Dakota had tasted or how good he had felt, she knew better than to get addicted to the wrong kind of man. The intensity of their attraction meant nothing in the scheme of things. Absolutely nothing.

Three

Dakota gazed around Annie's kitchen. Daisies popped out at him from everywhere. The wallpaper, towels and pot holders all displayed the white-and-yellow flower motif. Even the sunny-colored dining table sported a centerpiece sprouting silk replicas of the sissy blooms. The kitchen, he decided, along with the rest of the colorful house, had not been decorated with a man in mind.

The fifty-some-year-old ranch-style structure itself wasn't the problem. It offered plenty of windows, quality carpeting, fresh paint and well-crafted cabinetry. The master bathroom had been an addition, but it flaunted an antique claw-footed tub big enough for two. And the front porch presented a California-country view and an old-fashioned swing perfect for cuddling.

He looked over at Annie, who at the moment prepared dinner while bouncing Jamie, *their* two-year-old on her hip. Dakota shook his head. He actually had a wife and kids. *Him.* The confirmed bachelor.

Dakota scooped the tomato wedges he'd sliced into a wooden-style salad bowl and studied Jamie. The boy had a cherub's face, full and round with animated features. A mop of black hair, similar to his own, dusted the child's ears and fell upon his forehead in neatly sheared bangs. Jamie had attached himself to Annie like a clinging monkey, his big brown eyes watching Dakota's every move. The boy had been three months old when his parents died. Annie was the only mother he would ever remember.

When Dakota smiled and winked, the boy fisted Annie's T-shirt with chubby brown fingers and buried his face against her shoulder, tiny lips quivering in what looked like fright. Great. His son thought he was a two-headed monster in cowboy boots.

Annie stirred the simmering spaghetti sauce. "How's the salad coming?"

He glanced down at the bowl filled with a lush variety of fresh vegetables and fragrant herbs. She had an impressive little garden out back and plenty of room for a barn. Temecula, the small Southern California town in which Annie lived, offered sights, sounds and smells Dakota considered cowboy friendly. Its Old West history included the Pechanga Indians, the first of the Butterfield Overland Stages and turn-of-the-century cattle drives.

"Fine. About ready for the dressing."

She adjusted the wary child, opened a cabinet and removed a package mix. When she stood beside him arranging the ingredients, he reached for the vinegar bottle and their hands collided.

As a jolt of electricity shot up Dakota's arm, Annie staggered a little as though she too had been shocked. She snatched her hand back and they stared at each other.

Intently.

She moistened her lips, catching a strand of white-blond hair in the corner of her mouth. He swallowed. She brushed the silky lock away. He reached out to stroke her cheek. She shivered and closed her eyes.

He leaned in to kiss her, only to meet with resistance from the two-year-old still clutching her top.

"No!" Jamie pounded Dakota's shoulder. "Mommy mine."

With a guilty flush, Annie soothed and corrected the child all at once. "Oh, honey. Be nice to Kody. He wants to be your daddy."

Jamie scrunched his cherubic face in blatant disapproval, and Dakota's heart fell to the floor. Annie shook her head and carried the scowling child into the living room to watch TV with his brothers. When she returned to set the table, neither said a word.

A short time later they shared their first dinner as a family. Jamie, living proof of the stage Dakota had heard referred to as the "terrible twos," sat beside his mother, demanding her undivided attention.

The middle child, Miles, wiggled in his seat, humming as he twirled a glob of spaghetti around his fork. Miles's hair, cropped short and spiky on top, reminded Dakota of porcupine quills. Much to his relief, Miles accepted him without the slightest resistance. The talkative five-year-old seemed pleased to have a man in the house. Unlike Jamie, the older boys remembered him and understood his place in Jill's life. They'd spoken on numerous occasions about what Dakota had deemed the Dog Soldier Ceremony, the ritual that had made Jill his blood sister.

"Know what, Uncle Kody?" Miles asked, adding even more pasta to his already-packed fork.

"What?"

"Tye's getting a pair of glasses tomorrow. Funny-looking black ones. I'm glad I don't have to wear 'em. Don't want nobody callin' me four-eyes."

The boy in question, eight-year-old Tyler, stuck out his bottom lip in a gesture that hadn't decided whether to be a frown or a pout. He wore his wavy hair long and slicked back in kind of a fifties style. "I'm not a four-eyes."

Miles, the chatty porcupine, laughed. "You will be."

"Shut up!"

''No, *you*, shut up.''

Annie quieted them both with a stern look. Dakota made a mental note. If the kids act up, just glare at them.

She dabbed her lips with a paper napkin, a daisy-printed napkin. ''Miles, you know what I've told you about calling people names. And besides, there's nothing wrong with wearing glasses.''

Dakota watched Tyler tear apart a slice of garlic bread. Apparently he thought there was something wrong with having to wear glasses. His expression looked pained—a quiet child worried about looking different from his peers. Not many eight-year-olds wore glasses, Dakota supposed.

''Hey, how about you guys hanging out with me tomorrow instead of going to the baby-sitters?'' he suggested.

Miles said excitedly, ''Yeah! Can we, Annie-Mom? Can we?'' while his older brother barely managed a noncommittal shrug.

Annie turned to her husband with one of her stern looks. ''This might be a little soon.''

''No, it's not,'' Miles chimed in, his sauce-smeared mouth twitching in excitement. ''We want to hang out with Uncle Kody, don't we, Tye?''

Once again Tyler only shrugged.

Dakota sprinkled another layer of cheese over his spaghetti, his heart aching for the boy. ''You know, Tyler, I'd be glad to take you to the eye doctor tomorrow to pick up your glasses. Heck, I might even get a pair myself.''

The eight-year-old smiled for the first time that evening. ''*You* wear glasses?''

''Well…no, not exactly, but I've always thought they made guys look kinda smart…girls, too,'' he added, stealing a quick glance at Annie, who watched him curiously beneath her lashes. So what if he had twenty-twenty vision, Tyler seemed as though he needed a friend. ''Maybe I'll get a pair just like yours.''

''Really?'' Tyler's soulful eyes widened. ''Would you wear them all the time?''

''Sure. Why not?'' He wore sunglasses while he drove. A

regular pair probably wouldn't look or feel much different. And that smile on Tyler's face made him feel sort of warm and fatherly, as if he'd done and said the right thing.

When they finished dinner, the boys cleared their plates and went back into the living room. Dakota and Annie remained in the kitchen where they shared the task of rinsing dishes and loading them into the dishwasher. Dakota detested housework but felt obliged to help on his first night there.

She handed him the empty salad bowl. "You were wonderful with Tyler. He's had such a hard time since his parents died. He stresses about everything."

"It takes time to get over that kind of loss," Dakota responded, grateful he still had both of his parents. His folks supported him, no matter what he chose to do. They'd pretty much let him go his own way, recognizing his spirit for what it was. When he'd called and told them that he'd married Annie, they were shocked but pleased. They'd always considered her family. The kids, too.

Dakota wanted to be a good dad. Different from Annie's dad. Clay Winters had disappointed his daughter, often making promises he didn't keep. Dakota knew her childhood had been rocky at times. He assumed her devotion to Jill's boys had stemmed from her own tragedies. Annie had lost her mother to an illness three years before, so she had no one left but Mary and the kids. And now him. She had a husband, whether she wanted one or not.

Annie exited the kitchen to check on the boys, and Dakota stared out the window. He wasn't about to reveal the worries plaguing him. Could he make this marriage work? Become a good father? A proper husband? The kind of provider Annie and the kids deserved? He had to, he realized. This marriage was his Cheyenne duty, a responsibility he couldn't turn away from, no matter how much it scared him.

The first thing he needed to do, Dakota thought, was get settled in. Prove to his wife and children that he intended to stick around. He touched the windowpane and took a deep breath. Ignoring the covered patio, he focused on the uncultivated acres beyond. A barn was definitely in order. Maybe he'd look into one of those prefab models, hire a company that could put up a building right quick. Dakota had to find a way to establish roots, and his horses would help tie him to the land.

He stepped away from the window. He could renovate the inside of the house as well. The place was a bit small for five people, so a few additions wouldn't hurt. A man should look after his family, make them as comfortable as possible.

He rolled his shoulders and thought about Annie once again. She looked pretty tonight, sexy in an unpretentious way, wearing cotton shorts and tennis shoes, her tummy peeking out from beneath the shortened hem of a pastel T-shirt. She used to dress like that when she was a kid, too. A little girl in play clothes, feisty but feminine. Dakota smiled. Tiny Annie with her generous heart, always mooning after him.

His smile faded. She sure as heck wasn't mooning after him these days. Lovemaking didn't appear to be a priority in her mind.

As far as that went, Dakota decided, he'd have to give her some time and hope for the best. Of course, he'd still tease her the way he always had, laugh and act casual. Anything to keep her from knowing just how much her rejection hurt. He wasn't about to expose his wounded pride. No more brooding. From now on, he'd keep the ache inside.

Two hours later Annie tucked each child into bed with a prayer and a kiss, then went to her own room. She opened the door to find a shirtless Dakota leaning over the top drawer of her dresser, the one that contained her lingerie.

"What are you doing?" she snapped in a panic. He looked big and looming. Dangerous. Not at all like the surprisingly gentle man who had charmed Tyler over dinner, the man she'd started having dangerous fantasies about. For one crazy instant in the kitchen, she'd actually liked the idea of Dakota being her husband. But now, seeing him like this, she knew better. That dangerous side of him would never go away, that wild spirit that made men like him too much of a risk.

Dakota shot up and bumped his head on a brass floor lamp, knocking the scalloped shade askew.

Ignoring the lopsided lampshade, he stood to face her, clad in nothing but his underwear. Annie meant to look away but couldn't. Dakota's body had been sculpted for admiration. A broad, copper chest tapered to a washboard stomach, then moved to narrow hips and rock-hard thighs. The springy hair dusting his arms and legs managed to skip his chest, only to resume in a thin line that whorled around his navel.

Intrigued by the dark line that disappeared into the waistband of his Aztec-printed shorts, she blurted the first thing that came to mind. "You're wearing boxers. You had briefs on the other day."

A semblance of a smile floated across his lips. "I sleep in boxers. And how do you know what I was wearing the other day?"

"The top of your jeans were unbuttoned." Embarrassed that she'd commented on his personal attire, she felt a blush coming on. "I guess I noticed because I design underwear."

A slice of his hair connected with a raised eyebrow. "Do you design men's underwear, too?"

"No." She tugged on the front of her cropped T-shirt, suddenly wishing her own navel wasn't exposed. "Now what were you doing in the top drawer?"

He glanced back at the oak dresser. "Unpacking."

"But that's my drawer, with my things."

His seductive smile widened. Apparently he'd gotten a good glimpse of her lingerie preferences. "There weren't any empty ones, so I figured we could share. Is there a law against my things being next to yours?"

Thinking of his briefs next to her silk panties and demicup bras sent a forbidden tingle up and down her spine. "I'll clear a different drawer for you."

She strode past him, straightened the lampshade, then peered into the open drawer. As she removed his articles and placed them atop his duffel bag, several foil packets slipped out from the bundle.

Condoms? "What are these?" she asked stupidly.

Dakota knelt beside her, and damn if he didn't almost laugh. "If you don't know, squirt..."

Flustered, she picked up the colorful packets and smacked them into his palm. "Get rid of them."

As though dumfounded, he stared down at his hand. "But I always use protection."

Annie crossed her arms. "Well, your days of getting lucky are over. You don't need them anymore."

This time he actually had the gall to laugh. It rumbled from his chest like a quick blast of thunder. "All right. But you can't avoid me forever. We're married, ya know."

She pushed her lingerie drawer closed. "I was forced into this situation, remember?" As much as she appreciated him coming to her rescue, she wasn't about to be bullied into love-making. Nor did she want protection available for his convenience. "And stop laughing. This isn't funny."

He swallowed the last of his mirth and tossed the condoms back onto his duffel bag. "I'll get rid of them tomorrow."

"No. You'll throw them away right now," she said in her bossiest mom-voice. "And be sure to put them in the big trash can outside so the boys don't find them. Miles is obsessed with water balloons."

Dakota grabbed the packets, then burst back into laughter. "You don't really think...I mean...water balloons?"

Annie caught her husband's eye only to find herself humored right along with him. Miles was capable of all sorts of odd shenanigans. Dakota would find out soon enough. "Would you just get out of here and throw those away."

He tipped an imaginary cowboy hat and lunged to his feet. "Yes, ma'am."

She shook her head. The man hadn't even stopped to slip on a pair of jeans. What would the neighbors think if they saw him taking out trash in his underwear? Oh, good grief. What neighbors? The nearest house sat an acre away.

She cleared the middle drawer and shoved the previous contents into the bottom of her closet to deal with another time. Stretching, she rose to her feet and headed for the master bathroom. The kids were down, and Dakota's bed was made up on the couch. A much needed bubble bath and a warm bed with her favorite designer sheets awaited.

Twenty minutes later Annie emerged from the bathroom, her skin smoothed and scented, her body draped in a blush-rose nightgown—a modest yet feminine garment she had created for every mom who needed a little luxury in her life. Soft cotton swirled around her ankles, and a hint of lace added texture to a sweetheart bodice.

"I've been wondering what you sleep in."

Annie froze. Dakota, in her bed, dark and masculine amid the floral-printed sheets and hand-painted quilt. She resisted the urge to stroke her bare arms and the goose bumps chilling them. "What are you doing?"

"Admiring you. God, you're beautiful."

She ignored the compliment and the husky tone of his voice. "I made your bed up on the couch."

"I love blond hair. Especially yours. You remind me of one of those movie stars from a long time ago. Silvery-white hair and a body that won't quit."

Stop trying to seduce me. She pointed to the door. "Dakota. The couch."

He shook his head. "Sorry, darlin.' I had a spinal-cord injury. I can't sleep on the couch. Doesn't have proper back support." He glanced down at the sheet draped over his hips. "Does everything in your house have flowers on it? Daisies in the kitchen, roses in the bedroom..."

She began to pace. "Where am I supposed to sleep?"

He patted the space next to him and grinned. "Right next to your husband, darlin,' like a good little wife."

Annie blew an agitated breath. So Dakota had agreed to marry her and adopt the kids. That didn't mean she had to offer herself to him like a sacrificial lamb. If she gave him an inch, he'd surely take a mile. Or two. "Stop calling me *darlin.'* It's annoying." And kind of sexy. He had a drawl to die for.

"Sorry, dar—" A low chuckle sounded. "Honey."

Annie stopped pacing and stared down at him. There he was, his arms resting behind his head, looking like the king of Siam in her bed. Her comfortable, warm bed, with its extrafirm mattress and custom-ordered quilt. The sea-foam-and-mauve room had been decorated just to her liking. A rolltop desk and an antique headboard matched the whitewashed dresser. Lace curtains trimmed with a floral valance adorned both windows as baskets of potpourri sweetened the air. A mirrored vanity laden with perfume bottles sat adjacent to the bed—the very one Dakota lolled in.

She narrowed her eyes. "I should have found another Cheyenne to marry."

He grinned back at her. "You don't know any other Cheyenne men. Now quit acting like a baby and get in bed. I don't bite."

No, but he could turn her insides to mush with a kiss. And that scared the daylights out of her. "I'm not sleeping with you." She opened the closet and grabbed her robe. "I'll survive the couch."

"No way. That's not fair. Besides, if you sleep on the sofa every night, the kids will think we're fighting. And then they'll tell Harold."

Annie sighed. Dakota was right, of course. Harold had already called twice since they'd returned from Las Vegas. She certainly didn't want to create a problem in the older man's eyes. And she'd hate for the kids to think she and Dakota were fighting. Even though this marriage wasn't likely to last, she intended to keep Dakota as a friend. The screaming matches that had ended her parents' relationship still left her cold.

"Come on, squirt." Dakota moved closer to the wall, away from what he'd apparently decided was her side of the bed. "I'll be good. I swear. I won't even pester you for a good-night kiss."

"Fine. Let's just get some sleep." Annie hung her robe in the closet, turned off the light and climbed into bed without the slightest bit of ceremony. She needed to feign an air of indifference. He'd probably laugh if he knew how nervous she was.

Just as she closed her eyes, he rolled over, taking the blanket with him.

"Dakota!"

"What?"

"You're hogging the blanket."

The bed stirred as he sat up. "Sorry. Guess I'm not used to sharing."

Annie turned toward him, then swallowed her next breath. She should have let him keep the blanket. Moonlight trapped his silhouette, highlighting his movements. His hair tumbled forward as he plowed his hand through it, his extended arm perfectly formed.

She wasn't used to sharing, either. She had given up men years ago. Oh, right. *Now there's a sacrifice,* she thought ironically. *A virgin giving up men.*

They settled in once again, and she tried to keep herself from breathing too deeply. Deodorized soap lingered on his skin, a masculine scent she wasn't accustomed to. He must have showered in the bathroom the kids used.

Annie couldn't sleep. The king-size bed seemed suddenly too small. Dakota's brawn took up too much space, and her nervous stomach had decided to do cartwheels. As a crush-crazed adolescent, she used to marvel at his virility. Dakota was six years her senior, so when she had been an underdeveloped girl swooning over him, he'd stood tall and mature, teasing her about being a squirt. But at the time, his taunting hadn't deterred her crush. She used to think about him constantly, wishing he wasn't a bull rider. After the way her dad had lost his life, she couldn't help but worry about Dakota.

Did he miss the rodeo? she wondered. The thrill, the danger, the recognition. Annie twisted the satin hem on the blanket. The late nights. Easy women. His injury had forced him into retirement. He hadn't made that choice consciously.

"Annie?"

She startled at the sound of his voice. "What?"

"Now you're the one hogging the covers."

She released her grip. She had twisted the blanket so hard, she'd tugged it away from him. "Oh, sorry."

"Is something wrong?" he asked.

"I'm having trouble falling asleep," she admitted.

"Yeah, me, too. Being married is gonna take some getting used to, I suppose."

Not on her part. She didn't intend to get used to living with him. Not when she knew he'd find a reason to leave after the adoption.

"Do you like your new career?" she asked, changing the subject. She preferred to avoid the topic of marriage, especially while they shared a bed.

He shrugged. "Designing jewelry doesn't really feel like a career yet. I haven't sold many pieces."

"But you will. Your work is beautiful." The weight of her exquisitely crafted wedding band rested easily on her finger. He had talent, an instinctual gift.

"Thanks. I never expected it to be anything more than a hobby. But when I couldn't use my legs, I learned how to rely on my hands."

"They're great hands," she commented quickly, recalling how big and masculine they were, how safe they'd made her feel on the plane.

"You think so, huh?" A devilish sort of humor slipped into his tone. "I can do a lot more with them than just make jewelry. Hey, maybe I can give you a demonstration. You know, my hands, your body."

Annie smiled in spite of herself. "Is that all you think about?"

"It's tough not to when I'm married to someone who looks like you."

She rolled her eyes. "Nice try. But all these compliments you've been tossing my way aren't affecting me in the least."

Liar, a small voice in her head challenged.

Annie told it to shut up and raised the covers. He didn't need to know his words had stimulated her traitorous body. Her nipples felt like pebbles, hard and just a little bit achy.

Dakota plumped his pillow. "I'll probably be doing some traveling now and again. I thought I'd check out some of the finer Western stores on this coast. You know, to see if they might be interested in carrying my jewelry."

"You could get a sales rep," she suggested. "I'm sure

there's plenty of salesmen who'd be glad to promote a product from a well-known cowboy.''

"Yeah, I'd thought of that.'' Once again he raked his hand through his hair or she assumed he did by the movement of his arm. The moonlight had faded, darkening the room. "But I like being on the road, and I figured I'd go to a few powwows while I'm out there. You know, meet some other artists.''

Start a new life for himself on the road. It made sense. The gypsy cowboy. The gypsy artist. Just as she suspected, he was already finding excuses to be away from home. No doubt about it. This marriage wasn't about to last.

Annie sighed. Thank goodness she wasn't a crush-crazed kid anymore. Not falling for Dakota Graywolf would make his leaving a whole lot easier.

Dakota resisted the urge to cover his ears. Jamie had been bawling nonstop for the past twenty-five minutes, howling like a distressed coyote.

"Does he always do this after Annie-Mom leaves for work?'' he asked Miles.

"Nope,'' the boy replied. "He never cries at the baby-sitter's house.''

Dakota winced. The two-year-old, still dressed in his cartoon pajamas, stomped across the couch, screaming as he peered out the living room window. "Jamie just needs to get used to me,'' he said, repeating the same thing he'd told Annie earlier when she'd balked about leaving the youngest child with him.

"How long is that gonna take?'' Miles complained. "He's gettin' on my nerves.''

Dakota shrugged. He'd had the kids less than thirty minutes, and already the living room resembled the aftermath of a small explosion. Miles and Tyler's miniature car collection dominated the sand-colored carpet, along with every available pillow in the house. Since the boys were building a mountain range, he'd allowed them to haul in a few medium-size rocks. And although leaves and twigs hadn't been part of the deal, several makeshift trees grew from the pillow tops.

Dakota eyed the shrieking two-year-old. "Should I try another bottle?"

Tyler looked up from the construction-paper road he was creating. Up until now, the soft-spoken eight-year-old had remained quiet about his disgruntled little brother. "He likes candy."

"Really?" At this point, Dakota thought, Jamie could have anything he wanted. A pound of chocolate, a Cuban cigar, a new Porsche. "Do you have any candy in the house?"

Tyler and Miles exchanged a look. A we're-not-supposed-to-get-into-the-candy, Annie-Mom-will-get-mad look.

"C'mon you guys, this is an emergency."

Miles tore into the kitchen, and Dakota followed. "It's up there." The five-year-old pointed to a cabinet above the refrigerator.

Dakota reached up, thinking Annie must have used a chair to stash the goods. The top of her head barely reached his shoulder and this was a stretch even for him. He grabbed the yellow jar and peered into it. "Damn. I mean dang, there's all kinds of stuff in here. A Halloween variety."

"Uh-huh." Miles shifted his feet, his tongue darting in anticipation.

Dakota hid a smile and lowered the jar. "You want some?"

"Yeah." The boy grabbed a handful then called his brother. "Hey, Tye, come get some candy."

Tyler appeared instantaneously, telling Dakota he must have been lurking around the corner. Choosier than his brother, Tyler carefully picked through the jar. "Annie-Mom doesn't let us have too much at once," he said, sounding like eight going on thirty. Then again, he probably was. Dakota knew the boy had a near-genius IQ.

"Yeah," Miles chimed in. "Annie-Mom says candy makes us hyper."

"Makes *you* hyper," Tyler corrected. "Not me."

Dakota glanced down at the bouncing porcupine. How much more hyper could the kid get? "All right, what's Jamie's favorite?"

"Lollipops," came the joint reply.

Dakota ventured back into the living room, dodging cars, roads, trees and mountains. Approaching Jamie as cautiously as he would a man-shy colt, he held out a green lollipop.

The child gasped and hiccuped, his tear-lined eyes spying the candy. "Mine," he said, snatching the sucker and running to the corner of the sofa like a squirrel hoarding a five-pound nut. Dakota sank onto the opposite end of the couch and blew a relieved breath.

The older boys ate their candy, tossed the wrappers carelessly and resumed their car game while Dakota fingered the cigarettes in his front pocket. Annie had forbid him from smoking in the house. Unhealthy for the kids, she'd said.

"Hey, Miles, toss me one of those lollipops from the jar, would ya?"

Seconds later he caught the treat, winked at the kids, then silently cursed his tobacco habit. He popped the sucker into his mouth and checked out the furnishings to keep his mind off a cigarette. Already the lollipop was a poor substitute.

A prissy pink and teal color scheme dominated the room. Although he appreciated the heavy oak coffee table and functional entertainment center, the sofa and chairs would have to go, along with all the fake posies. And what was with the frilly lace things hanging on the walls? For crying out loud, boys lived there.

Deciding a brown leather sofa and some sturdy recliners would "man" the place up a bit, Dakota ran his hand along the floral-print upholstery.

"Did somebody spill something on the couch?" he asked, encountering a damp spot.

The engine noises ceased, but Miles continued to drive a tow truck over the rocks. "Maybe Jamie dumped his bottle."

"Or wet his pants," Tyler added.

As Dakota glanced over at the two-year-old, the boy moved closer to the window, protecting his lollipop like a pacifier. His bottom did appear damp. "He's not potty trained?"

Miles shrugged. "He's just learning. Most times he forgets."

Oh, hell. Annie didn't mention diapers. Or did she? Dakota

scratched his chin. What did she say this morning? While she'd clucked around the kitchen like a mother hen in high heels, he'd sipped his coffee and struggled to absorb her version of his parental duties. Problem was she had bombarded him with too much information, too many rules to follow. Finally he'd just tuned her out, deciding to enforce his own brand of parenting.

He caught sight of Jamie's bottom again. "Where's the diapers?" he asked.

"Jamie, go get your trainers," Tyler ordered, barely glancing up.

The little one crawled off the couch and ran down the hall. While he was gone, Dakota noticed the candy jar seemed a might low. Apparently Miles had been indulging himself. When Jamie returned, he carried what appeared to be a pair of disposable underwear.

An hour and three lollipops later, father and sons left the house and the mess they'd made. Jamie's fluffy black mop hadn't been combed and his shirt rode backward, but Dakota felt proud nonetheless. The boy's tennis shoes were triple tied, and he wasn't bawling. It was a start.

Dakota herded his brood into the optometrist's office, feeling a bit bleary-eyed and in desperate need of a smoke. Luckily the woman behind the counter turned out to be an experienced grandmother. She fussed over a slightly cranky Jamie and praised Dakota when a sugar-induced Miles bragged about their new "cowboy" dad. "He's adoptin' us," the boy had said with a crooked, chocolate smile.

They settled onto the chrome chairs that lined the counter and waited for Louise, the silver-haired grandma, to fit Tyler with his new glasses. The well-lit, spacious building sported mirrored walls and tall, white cylinders filled with assorted frames.

After Louise stepped back, Tyler turned to Dakota with an uncertain expression. "Do they look funny?"

He grinned. The kid had chosen black horned-rimmed glasses. Fifties style, just like his hair. "No. They're sharp. I like 'em."

The boy glanced back at the mirror. "Do you think I look like Buddy Holly?"

Dakota startled. "Are you sure you're only eight? Buddy Holly was even before my time."

"Our dad used to play his songs all the time. He liked that kind of music." Tyler fingered the glasses. "Even Miles remembers. He knows all the words to 'Peggy Sue'."

I'll bet you know the words, too, Dakota thought, swallowing the lump in his throat. "Yeah, you look like Buddy Holly. Real fifties-like." He reached over and smoothed the boy's gelled hair. "I'm sure your dad would approve."

"You're getting a pair like mine, right?"

Dakota nodded. "Yep. Just like 'em."

When Louise brought the frames and promised they could be filled with a blank prescription within an hour, he slipped them on and stared at his reflection, stunned by the transformation.

Lord have mercy.

Peggy Sue, darlin', brace yourself 'cause here I come, cowboy boots and all.

Four

Annie held her hand out. "Come sit by me."

Dakota abandoned the redwood chair and made a beeline for the swing. Relaxing on the porch at 10 p.m. was nice, but sharing the swing with his pretty blond wife was even better. He settled onto the wooden seat and inhaled her sweet scent. She smelled cleaner than the night air, like rainwater, citrus shampoo and rose petals.

She tilted her head. "Put your glasses on."

Nothing like ruining a romantic moment, Dakota thought. He knew the horned-rimmed style didn't suit him. He reached into his shirt pocket and slid the black frames onto his face. He looked like a nerdy fifties version of Clark Kent in the dang things.

Annie, of course, looked beautiful. She lounged in a white floor-length cotton dress, the neckline decorated with silver embroidery and tiny mirrors. He'd seen similar clothes in an import shop, the kind that sold candles, ivory elephants and wicker furniture. Suddenly he wondered if her fragrances were imported, too. The glass-blown bottles that contained them certainly emitted an exotic allure.

She leaned in close and gently brushed her lips across his. Stunned by the affection, he missed the opportunity to slide his hands into her hair and deepen the kiss, taste her with his tongue.

"That was for making Tyler happy about wearing glasses."

Dakota fingered his own self-consciously. "He looks cute in them. Hell of a lot better than I do."

"That's not true. I think they make you look kind of sexy. Studious and wild all at once."

He grinned. "Maybe I should start wearing white T-shirts and roll a pack of smokes up in the sleeve."

"And buy a motorcycle," she suggested in a teasing tone.

"I had a Harley in high school, remember? A '59 Duo-Glide. Restored it myself."

Annie shook her head, spilling luxurious platinum locks over her shoulders and down her arms. "How could I forget? That thing was noisy."

Dakota lowered his glasses. "Yeah, but it was fast. I like to move fast and get whipped around." He nudged her shoulder. "What about you, darlin'? You interested in going for a rough ride? Or would you prefer it slow and easy?"

In an overdramatized feign of innocence, she pushed his glasses back into place. "We're talking Harleys, right?"

He chuckled. Boy, it felt good to flirt.

They rocked the swing and stared at the landscape. A warm breeze whispered through the trees, rustling leaves and stirring grass. Stars winked from a moonlit summer sky and sprinkled magic over the flowers lining the stone walkway. Dakota smiled, feeling as though he'd been swept back in time to an era filled with stolen kisses, leather jackets, milk shakes and innocence. Maybe his glasses weren't so bad after all.

"Dakota?"

"Hmm?"

"I'm really impressed with the way you handled the boys today. They ate a healthy lunch, the house was spotless and you even got some of your own work done."

"Oh, yeah, thanks." He swallowed his guilt. Did fast food and a pound of candy fall under the category of a healthy lunch? Avoiding her gaze, Dakota rocked the swing a little faster. "They're good kids. No trouble." The spotless house had come via a cleaning lady he'd found through a local advertisement. And as far as getting work done—he'd been in the garage unpacking silver equipment while the boys were making the mess he'd paid the good-humored maid twice her rate to clean.

"I can't believe Jamie actually took a nap. He never naps for me."

Dakota slowed the swing. Well, hell's bells, the kid had worn himself out from bawling half the day. "Must have been the lullaby."

She cocked her head. "You sang to him?"

Dakota bit back a grin. He'd put the boy behind the crib bars and crooned out a pitiful version of "Jailhouse Rock." Jamie had stuck his padded bottom in the air and covered his head with a blanket, quickly giving Dakota his opinion of the sorry Elvis impersonation. "Yep, worked like a charm."

"So Jamie's comfortable around you now?"

Are you kidding? He won't come near me unless I give him a lollipop. "Well, ya know, we're working on it."

Annie arched her back. "I had a tough time getting Miles to sleep tonight. I guess he was just overly excited about spending the day with you."

"Yeah, that was probably it." *That and all the sugar.* Dakota glanced up at the porch roof. "What do you say we turn in? I'm beat."

She nodded and took the hand he offered. After locking the front door, they checked on the sleeping children, smiled at each other the way parents did, then went to their own room.

Dakota used the bathroom first, undressed and tossed his clothes into the hamper while Annie gathered her nightgown. Five minutes later, still wearing his glasses, he crawled into bed, and she entered the bathroom. When she returned, he adjusted the covers and moistened his lips. Tonight she wore a thin-strapped gown that matched her eyes. Although the simple garment flaunted no adornment, the pale gold fabric and the way it clung to her figure caused a carnal awakening in him. The faint outline of her breasts sent a surge of heat straight to his groin.

Rather than joining him in bed, she sat on the skirted stool in front of the vanity and picked up a lotion bottle. He braced his back against a pillow and admired the graceful way in which she moved. Since the vanity sat adjacent to the foot of the bed, he had an unobstructed view of his wife and her reflection.

As she poured the scented lotion into her palm and began smoothing it up and down her arm in a slow, fluid motion, Dakota's hunger intensified. By the time she repeated the process on her other arm, he pictured her naked, an erotic fairy-tale princess, white-blond hair tumbling over the bed. In his mind's eye, mouths tasted and bodies joined, tongue thrusts matched hip thrusts, teeth nipped, scents mingled....

"Dakota?"

Her voice nearly sent him and his guilt-ridden lust flying off the bed. "What?"

When she turned toward him, he realized she must have caught his reflection in the glass. Without realizing it, he'd managed to align himself with the mirror.

"Are you okay? You look strange."

For a moment he just stared. Could she really be that naive, that unaware of her sensuality? "Are you going to brush your hair?" he asked.

Annie tilted her head. "Why? Is the light bothering you?"

"No." He pushed the floral-dotted covers away. "I just thought that if you were going to brush your hair, that maybe I could do it for you."

A curious expression crossed her face. "That seems like an odd thing for you to want to do."

Damn it, woman, don't you know how much I need to touch you? "Jamie fussed when I tried to comb his hair today so I figured maybe I was a bit rough or something. I thought I could practice on you."

She nibbled her bottom lip, something he'd seen her do

when debating an issue in her mind. "I don't know, Da-kota—"

"Come on," he persisted. "I'm new at this dad thing and I've never brushed anyone's hair but my own. And mine's so messy, I have to be rough." He pulled a hand through the unruly mass. "Hell, half the time I wonder why I even bother."

A soft smile contradicted the uncertainty in her eyes. "Maybe I should be the one brushing your hair instead."

"Another time." He bounded off the bed and stood behind her. Tonight he intended to slide his fingers through those luxurious blond strands. Dakota removed his glasses, placed them on the vanity and grasped the silver-backed brush. With an appreciative eye, he examined the fine detail.

She watched him trace a finger over the ornate engraving. "It belonged to my mother. That and the perfume bottles are about the only family heirlooms I have."

He lifted the brush to her hair. "It's beautiful." Gently, he placed the bristles against her scalp and slid them down the length of the silken tresses. Her hair flowed with each stroke, cascading to the center of her back.

Inhaling the strawberry-spiced lotion rising from her skin, he moved closer. With an impatient curse, he damned her beauty, the heat of the moment and the painful need swelling his loins. She met his gaze in the mirror and the words in his head spilled from his lips. "Darlin,' why won't you make love with me?"

Annie's heart hammered against her chest. "Because I was forced into this marriage. And, in a sense, so were you." Why did he have to be so ruggedly appealing? Dakota Graywolf had been bred to command a stallion, protect his sons, pleasure a woman. The abrupt angle of his cheekbones and harsh cut of his jaw had descended from a long line of warriors, as did powerful limbs and strong, artistic hands. His nostrils flared as he indulged in the fragrance of her hair. No man had ever touched her so simply yet so erotically.

"But we're attracted to each other, Annie. Isn't that enough?"

She hugged herself through a shuddering breath. He didn't understand, but then how could he? He slept with women like Sheila Harris. "I'm not as free as you, Dakota. I can't be with someone out of sheer lust. We've never even been on a date."

A mischievous grin twitched his lips. "If you want to date, then we'll date. I'll ask Mary to watch the kids this weekend. I'll buy you flowers, we'll go to dinner…"

Annie trapped his gaze. "I don't make love on the first date so wipe that smirk off your face."

"Spoilsport." He pulled the brush through the ends of her hair. "Do you at least kiss on the first date?"

"Sometimes." The humor inside her died quickly. She turned to face him. "We shouldn't make light of this, Dakota. Over 50 percent of all marriages fail these days. And since most of those people wanted to get married, I'd say that makes our situation pretty hopeless." She was giving him an out, she realized, making it easy for him when the time came for him to leave.

He skimmed a callused finger across her cheek. "Darlin,' can't you just live for the moment? Enjoy what each day brings?"

No. She couldn't. Richard had been a live-for-the-moment type and his freewheeling actions had made mincemeat out of her heart. She turned back to the mirror. "This conversation is going nowhere."

He resumed brushing her hair. "So we won't talk about being together. But I guarantee you, Annie, it will happen. And when it does, it will be the most incredible, sensual experience of our lives."

She wet her lips nervously. If he only knew how many times she'd wondered what making love with him would be like. Annie adored the old movie classics, and in his own way, Dakota mastered the epitome of a matinee-idol rogue. Daring, sexy, self-assured. And just like the celluloid heroes, he even had a sense of humor. Of course none of that mattered because movies were make-believe, and real-life rogues cheated as often as they charmed. Sleeping with him would be a mistake.

A glorious mistake, she suspected. His touch felt like a slice of heaven. Intimate and gentle. "You should consider becoming a hairdresser. You're really good at this."

He chuckled. "Don't let my old rodeo buddies hear you say that. I have an image to uphold, ya know."

"Nothing could hurt your image." He was the cowboy who beat the odds. The one who stood tall and walked again. Everything he did, he did with passion.

"Don't tell anyone," he said, nuzzling her neck, "but I know how to make shampoo. My mom taught Mary and me all kinds of natural stuff. Goes along with the heritage, I suppose. Can't be a good Cheyenne if you don't know how to survive off the land."

An enthralling image invaded her mind. Ponderosa pines, clear blue water and a naked warrior lathering his hair. What a fantasy.

Annie frowned at her reflection. She better avoid that fantasy at all costs. Her naked warrior looked a bit too much like Dakota. A man who lived for the moment. A man who would make love to her, then move on, eager for the next blonde who came his way. A blonde who wore tight dresses and bright-red nail polish, just like Sheila Harris.

Saturday morning. Annie punched the button on the shrieking alarm clock, immediately sensing Dakota wasn't beside her. Within two weeks time, she'd come to know the deep timbre of his breathing and scent of his deodorized soap.

Yawning, she tumbled out of bed. French-roasted coffee percolated in the kitchen, the rich aroma slipping into the room like a stream of cartoon smoke tapping her shoulder. Young, excited voices chatted and giggled. Plates and silverware clanked and rattled.

Annie reached for her favorite mom-appropriate robe, a thick peach-colored chenille. Her other favorites, spun from the finest silk, were cataloged with hues such as champagne-blush and raspberry-froth. Lingerie had become an obsession since she'd hooked her first training bra.

The kitchen buzzed with activity. Her children nibbled on happy-face pancakes, one of Mary Graywolf's breakfast spe-

cialties. Sliced strawberries made up the mouths, raisins provided beady little eyes. Depending on the ingredients available,
the food features often changed. The expression, however, did
not.

Annie kissed the top of each child's head and accepted a
raisin eyeball from Jamie, who'd already squished half the
smile between his fingers. Tyler appeared concerned about disturbing the face and had consequently nibbled around it. Miles,
of course, had drenched his in syrup.

Annie smiled at the woman flipping another flapjack. "Hi,
Mary. Did you make a pancake for me?"

"Coming right up." Mary's signature braid spun as she
moved, her long sturdy body clothed in a Hawaiian-print
blouse and denim shorts.

Annie received a small stack with the same smiling face
perched precariously on top. Her coffee was already on the
table. "This was a nice surprise. I wasn't expecting you."

Mary prepared her own plate then sat beside Tyler. "Dakota
asked me to watch the kids today. He said something about
both of your salesgirls at the boutique calling in sick."

Normally Annie didn't work at the shop on Saturdays, even
if it was Intimate Silk's busiest retail day. Weekends were for
the boys, at least the daylight hours. Saturday and Sunday eve-
nings were often spent in the den she'd converted into a sewing room. The rest of the week included managing the shop
and designing custom pieces for an eclectic clientele that included successful businesswomen, fashion models and mis-
tresses of short, bald wealthy old men. She treated everyone
with respect, regardless of her opinion of their life-style. Sometimes even the wives of the wealthy old men patronized her
boutique, often with a handsome gigolo in tow. Her favorite
customers, of course, were the happily married who enjoyed
enticing their husbands.

"I guess Dakota made other plans," Annie said. Since both
of her salesgirls had the flu, she had no choice but to open the
shop this morning. Last night Dakota had agreed to watch the
kids since their regular baby-sitter wasn't available.

Mary shrugged. "I don't know. He just said you needed a sitter."

Miles looked up from his plate, licking his lips. "Aunt Mary's taking us to the zoo today."

Annie sipped her coffee. "That's great, honey." Soon they'd have their own zoo. Construction was already underway on a barn and roping arena. Dakota was anxious to get his horses settled in, and a roping arena meant steers. She'd bought a house with acreage so the kids could have a pony. A miniranch she hadn't counted on.

Miles piped up again. "Uncle Kody said we could get a pig."

"A pig?"

"Yeah, the kind with a potbelly. And he's gonna make our house bigger so me and Tye won't have to share a room no more."

"Finally." Tyler adjusted his glasses. "Miles is a slob."

"Am not!"

"Are, too."

"Boys," Annie corrected, quieting them instantly. Pushing her plate away, she frowned. Why was she always the last to know what her husband's plans were? "Where is Uncle Kody?"

"Outside," Miles said. "He's smoking."

She turned to Mary. "I'll be back in a few minutes."

Annie found her husband in the backyard, standing amid the dawn. Although a burst of yellow illuminated an azure sky, it wasn't warm enough to heat the ground. Morning dew glittered across tall blades of grass, chilling her bare toes.

With the backdrop of a partially constructed barn, Dakota resembled the cowboy that he was, his hat dipped low, a cigarette dangling from the corner of his mouth. He leaned against the redwood fence that separated the patio from the rest of the property, one booted foot propped on a cross board. The rolled-up sleeves of a faded-denim shirt exposed bronzed forearms, and well-worn jeans hugged a taut, masculine rear.

When Annie ventured closer, he caught sight of her and

quirked a lazy smile, the cigarette curling smoke in the brisk morning air. She tightened her robe.

"Why didn't you tell me you were planning to add on to the house?" she asked, feeling possessive of her home. From the first day this man had moved in, he'd begun rearranging her life. Sharing a bathroom with him wasn't easy, either. He left the cap off the toothpaste, wrinkled the hand towels and never put the toilet seat back down.

Dakota drew on the cigarette, and although she couldn't see his eyes beneath the low-riding Stetson, she knew they appraised her with cool reserve. Her defensive tone would have been hard to miss.

Exhaling, he lifted his chin. "You have a problem with the boys having their own room?"

"No." Annie looked back at a lawn chair, considered sitting, then reconsidered. She hated looking up to him as it was. Being seated would put her at more of a disadvantage. "But I have a problem with you making decisions without consulting me first. This is my house."

"And I'm your husband and the children's father. My role is to provide for the family. So if I think the house needs more rooms, I'll add them. I'm not taking your home away, I'm improving it."

Gee, he had an answer for everything. "What about the pig?"

He flicked ashes over the fence. "I've heard they make good pets."

Annie resisted the urge to dig below the grass and fling a handful of dirt at him. He had that cocky smirk on his face, the one he used to wear when she was a foolish little girl who had worshipped the ground he walked on. "What's wrong with the usual dog variety?"

"Nothing. I already told the boys they could each have one."

Her mouth dropped. "And who's going to feed and pick up after three dogs?"

The shrinking cigarette bobbed. "The kids are."

Oh, right. That would last a day. Dakota was still inexperienced where the children were concerned. "It won't happen. You and I will get stuck with the pooper-scooper."

He smirked again. "I've shoveled manure all my life, dar-lin'. But I'm not worried about the boys. They'll do their share. Sure, Jamie's still too young, but Tye and Miles promised to look after his pup."

"Tyler and Miles promise not to whine at bedtime, but that hasn't stopped them."

"A boy should have a dog," he said. "And a horse."

Annie jammed her fists into her pockets. "Please don't tell me you promised them each their own pony."

"Nope." Dakota extinguished the cigarette, then flicked it over the top rail. "They're not getting ponies. Ponies are rarely broke properly. Not enough cowboys small enough to do the job. I'm getting them a horse, the best one I can find."

She raised a hand above her head. "A big, huge horse?"

"Uh-huh. A well-broke, well-trained, loyal old gelding. My kids aren't learning to ride on some ill-mannered little pony. Besides, Tyler's beyond the pony stage. He's old enough for some serious riding."

Dakota was right, of course. She had been locked into the pony idea because her father had promised her one when she was little. A pony for his princess. Yeah, right. She never got one, nor did he ever teach her to ride. Mary and Jill had taught her long after her dad had died. "Is there anything else you've neglected to tell me?"

"Yeah." He tipped the Stetson and unmasked his midnight eyes. "Since you're shy a salesperson at your boutique, I'm going to work with you today."

Please, Lord, tell me he didn't say what I thought he did. "I sell lingerie, Dakota."

"I know. But you said Saturdays were busy and you've been running yourself ragged all week. I can unload stock or something. Besides, I'm curious to see the place."

"So meet me for lunch some afternoon. I don't need you hanging around all day."

"I know damn well that you've got merchandise that needs unloading. I heard you talking to one of the salesgirls on the phone about it. And if you keep pushing yourself like you have been, *you'll* end up with the flu.'' He lowered his foot from the cross board. ''I'm going with you whether you like it or not.''

She gritted her teeth. Once again he dictated her life. ''You work as many hours as I do.''

''Yeah, but I'm coping better than you are. Half the time you look as if you're sleepwalking.''

''That's because your snoring keeps me up.'' No way would she admit fighting her attraction to him was the true cause of her exhaustion.

His dark eyes narrowed. ''I don't snore.''

True, he didn't. She'd only said it to aggravate him. He breathed heavily while he slept. Sexy and husky. ''My customers won't appreciate a man hanging around.''

''I'll stay out of the way.''

He'd better, she thought, because some of her customers would find this macho cowboy much too scrumptious. Turning on her bare heel, she strode back to the house. Saying no was getting harder and harder. And damned if he didn't know it.

Five

——

Intimate Silk was located a block from the ocean on Pacific Coast Highway, cozied between an Italian bistro and a French bakery. Annie thought it belonged there. In her opinion, women's lingerie was as much of a treat as the kind with calories. Pasta *primavera,* chocolate éclairs and lace teddies made a delicious trio.

Dakota seemed to think so, too. He hadn't quit smiling since he'd entered the boutique, and the only word he'd managed thus far was an awestruck "Damn."

A vintage bar stocked with champagne and juice dominated one wall. Brass fixtures displaying intimate apparel enticed from all angles of the room. Several 1930s black-and-white glamour portraits featured leggy starlets draped in satin and wrapped in long, flowing boas. Plush carpet, the color of Annie's favorite blush zinfandel, padded the floors.

The front counter was stocked with strands of pearls, gauntlet gloves, rhinestone bracelets, garter belts and thigh-high nylons, with and without seams. Baskets of scented toiletries were artfully arranged throughout the store.

Dakota took in everything, Annie noticed. Absorbed every detail. "Can I sleep here tonight?" he asked with a mischievous grin.

His approval pleased her. Rugged cowboy or not, the man had an artistic eye. She pointed to a Victorian-style sofa. "Be my guest."

He declined in a sexy drawl. "Doesn't look big enough for two." Striding over to the display case, he peered inside, then tapped on the glass above the garter belts. "Do you ever wear one of these?"

Annie toyed with a button on her jacket. Today she'd chosen a white suit and ebony camisole. The oversize jacket worked well with the split skirt and basic black pumps. "I have one on now."

"Damn." He tunneled all ten fingers through his hair, then roamed the length of her with predator eyes. "Raise your skirt."

Oh, my God. "No."

"Show me."

"Dakota, I'm at work."

He moved closer. "The store isn't even open yet. The door's still locked."

A wicked sensation fluttered in her midsection. A part of her wanted to show him. "I can't."

A small smile played over his lips. "Yes, you can. Besides you want to."

"I do not," she lied with an indignant huff. "You don't know the first thing about what I want."

"Fine. Be that way." He gestured toward the door leading to the stockroom. "Why don't you show me what needs to be done so I can get to work."

The stockroom was also her sewing and design area, so she kept it bright and orderly. The walls and cement floor wore a recent coat of white paint. Her drawing table, several headless dress forms, a compact desk and a prized sewing machine occupied one half of the room while a small lunch table, a rolling rack and stock equipment dominated the other. A tiny but spotless rest room sported fuzzy, pink, toilet tank and lid covers.

"You have a drawing table and sewing machine at home," Dakota noted.

"Sometimes I have to bring my work home. There just doesn't seem to be enough hours in the day."

He walked over to one of the dress forms and stared at the bustier hugging the inanimate body. "Pretty hot."

"Thanks." The hand-beaded, white satin garment was part of a trousseau. Boned for shape, it dipped low in front and cross-laced in back like a corset. The future bride for whom it was designed had perfect-shaped breasts and legs up to her chin. Her breasts had been cosmetically enhanced but the legs boasted of lucky genes. "It's time consuming, but I enjoy it. Making specialty items is how I got started."

He advanced to the other side of the room, lifted one of the boxes and opened it with a utility knife. "How much of the stock do you actually sew yourself?"

She watched him remove a baby-doll pajama set. "Only the custom pieces. Most of the regular stock is manufactured at a design house downtown. The rest I buy from other companies."

Eyeing the pastel pajamas with a faint smile, he hung them carefully on the rack. She explained how to price and tag the garments and where to file the packing slip. Dakota's efficiency didn't surprise her. She'd observed him at home in the garage, working diligently. He crafted his jewelry with patient, agile hands. Each piece seemed to reflect a part of him—a mix of cowboy and American Indian roots. She'd also discovered he had a good business sense. He'd invested his past earnings well and had already started trust funds for the children.

Annie smoothed her lapel. She'd opened Intimate Silk on an inheritance from her mother, a woman who'd worked hard and saved all her life. Annie had learned firsthand how even a small amount of money could improve one's life. She wanted that and more for her children. The boys were her heart and soul.

"It's almost time to open the store," she said. "I'll clear some display racks for the new stock."

He barely glanced up. "Okay. I'll bring it out when its tagged and ready to go."

"Dakota?"

"Hmm?"

"Thanks."

This time his eyes met hers. "You're welcome, squirt. You've got a nice place here."

She smiled and headed for the front door, keys in hand. The man's penetrating gaze had stirred the butterflies in her stomach. Lately it seemed the winged creatures were constant companions.

By noon, Annie's third customer of the day swept through the entryway, dripping diamonds in her wake. Maddie Ferguson, a fiftyish flamboyant redhead, headed straight for the bar, splashed a drop of orange juice into a glass then topped it with champagne.

"Hello, sugar." She flashed Annie a cosmetic smile, straight and white. For someone her age, Maddie had a terrific body—long, lean and toned. A former beauty queen who'd married an elderly oil tycoon, she'd been widowed before her twenty-ninth birthday. Currently she dabbled in art and real estate—Picasso and beach-front apartment buildings.

"You look great," Annie said, meaning it. Not many women could wear white leggings, no bra, an emerald silk blouse and shiny gold sandals with a giant handbag to match.

"You think?" Maddie ran a manicured, diamond-studded hand down her curves. "I've been working out like crazy." She tossed a loose wave behind her ear. Maddie's hair was short but full of body. "And I hate to sweat. Any woman who claims she enjoys peddling her rear off on an exercise bike is a liar."

Annie smiled. "A new man?" The redhead loved skimpy lingerie almost as much as she loved virile young men.

Maddie sipped her champagne. "What else? If there were no men in the world, I'd stay in bed and eat bonbons all day."

Annie differed. She exercised for herself, men had nothing to do with it. The same with indulging in fancy lingerie—she liked the feeling of silk against her body and lace made her feel special. She'd never been one to seek male approval.

"Speaking of men…" The other woman's green eyes followed Dakota across the room.

Annie hadn't even realized he'd come onto the sales floor. The moment she saw him, her tummy unleashed a few more butterflies. His broad shoulders and faded denims appeared exceptionally rugged amid the feminine frills. And although he looked out of place, he stocked the merchandise with efficiency, as though he'd done it a hundred times before.

A coy smile tilted Maddie's collagen-filled lips. "Your new toy, sugar?"

He'd like to be. "Dakota's my husband."

"My, my, but you do have taste. Hmm. He doesn't look like the marrying kind. You must have done something special to rope that one."

Annie tried not to frown. "Of course." *We're adopting the same children.*

Maddie eyed Dakota again. "Nothing like a real live cowboy to get a girl's juices flowing. That sexy glitch in his walk means rodeo. Right?"

"Former bull rider. NFR world champ."

"Top of the line." The redhead winked. "Being Texas born and bred, I've ridden a few cowboys in my time. And they are yummy." As Dakota moved to another display rack, she cocked her head. "Say, sugar, he isn't by any chance that Native American bull rider who got trampled, is he? I read about him somewhere. That guy was hurt pretty bad."

Annie nodded. "Dakota Graywolf. That's him."

"Well, he sure is looking fine now."

"My husband's a very determined man. And a talented one, too. He's a jewelry designer."

Maddie moistened her lips. "Jewelry? As in diamonds?"

The businesswoman in Annie snapped back into focus. Maddie loved jewelry even more than lingerie or men. Annie lifted her wrist and modeled a bracelet she'd borrowed from Dakota's collection. Although most of his jewelry presented sterling silver and turquoise, this piece flaunted white gold, lapis and diamonds. Contemporary inlay and quality stones combined with traditional etching made it an exquisite creation.

Maddie's green eyes grew hungry as she reached a hand out.

"It's for sale," Annie offered.

"What about the ring?"

Annie curled her fingers. "That's my wedding band."

"Oh, sorry." The other woman batted a set of artificial lashes. "I'll take the bracelet," she said, without asking the price. "Just add it to the rest of my purchases." After handing Annie her empty champagne glass, she appraised a black mesh teddy. "Time to shop."

Two hours and nearly twenty-eight hundred dollars later, Maddie Ferguson sashayed out the door, blowing Annie a Texas-style kiss.

Elated yet exhausted, Annie invited Dakota to share lunch with her at the bar. "I don't normally eat on the sales floor, but I figured I'd make an exception for today."

He poured her a glass of sparkling cider, popped open a soda for himself, then unwrapped the sandwiches he'd purchased at a local deli. Annie had ordered sliced turkey, no mayo, extra tomatoes. Dakota had opted for roast beef smothered in avocado.

After swallowing an aggressive bite, he smiled. "Best thing California has to offer."

She assumed he referred to the guacamole. "I'd say the beach is a close second."

"Yeah, all those blondes in their string bikinis."

"I was talking about the sand and the ocean." Annie jabbed him with her elbow. "Besides, you're not supposed to notice other women."

He chuckled. "I'm married, not dead, darlin'."

Although he'd made the remark with a teasing twinkle in his eye, she couldn't seem to quell the jealousy pangs. After Dakota had finished stocking the new merchandise, he'd explored Pacific Coast Highway—claiming he'd wandered in and out of antique stores, vintage shops, retail boutiques and eateries.

Apparently, she thought with a grimace, he'd also taken in the bikini-clad blondes. "What do you really think of California?"

"I'm learning to appreciate it. I have to admit that Old Town Temecula's a cowboy's dream. And then, of course, there's the beach." He motioned in a grand gesture. "Regardless, though, I'm keeping my cabin in Montana. The boys will love it."

Who wouldn't, Annie thought. Dakota's cabin consisted of one large room with a stone fireplace, a wood burning stove, a rustic bed and some leather chairs. It managed to be primitive and homey, a bachelor's retreat, with a stream that ran through the property.

Annie twisted her ring. Apparently Dakota intended to return to his cabin someday. Adding on to her house and building a barn didn't mean he planned on staying in California forever. Should it matter? she asked herself. Dakota would still be there for the boys. Plenty of men were weekend fathers.

She picked at her sandwich while Dakota devoured his. She had gotten used to living her life without a man. Annie Winters had learned independence long ago. When Dakota Graywolf was ready to move on, she'd let him. Being alone was a lot safer that losing her heart.

Women, Dakota thought, were a stubborn breed. By Monday evening his overworked wife had ended up with a strong dose of the flu.

She mumbled something through the thermometer he'd jammed under her tongue. Something that sounded like, "Don't you dare say 'I told you so.'"

He crossed his arms and peered down at her. *Well, I did.*

Somehow she managed to look frail and belligerent at the same time. Although the bed and all its puffy lace nearly swallowed her whole and shadows dogged her eyes, an obstinate expression shone through.

When the digital thermometer beeped, he grabbed it before she could. "Still 102. You're not leaving this bed."

"But Jamie's crying. He won't understand." She pushed the covers away. "I have to explain to him that Mommy's sick."

Dakota yanked the sheet back up, then tucked it around her. "*I'll* explain that you're sick. And he's with his brothers so there's no logical reason for him to be bawling. He latches on to you like a clinging vine. That can't be normal."

"That's because he's jealous of you." She stared up at him, her jaw defensively set. "I'm the only parent he's ever known. He was three months old when his mom and dad died."

"I know all that." Dakota sighed. Annie could argue about the same thing for hours. "But spoiling him rotten isn't helping the situation any. He's going to have to accept the fact that he has two parents now."

She swallowed and winced as if her throat hurt. "But—"

"But nothing. If you go talk to him, he'll only cry harder when you go back to bed. Besides, you'll expose him to the flu. Then the other two will get it." *And I'll be making chicken soup and playing nursemaid for the next two weeks.* He'd already cooked up one batch. Nobody could call him a helpless man. He couldn't clean worth a damn, but he knew how to make homemade soup.

"What time is it?" she asked.

Dakota stifled a laugh. He'd wrapped her in bed so tight, she could barely turn her head to see the clock. "It's after ten. I've got to get the kids down. They should have been tucked in hours ago."

"Where are you sleeping?"

"On the couch. One or two days won't hurt me." He had exaggerated about not being able to sleep on the sofa, but now wasn't the time to bring that up. "Close your eyes, darlin'. I'll take care of Jamie."

"Okay," she whispered in a fading voice.

Dakota loosened her bedding and checked the nightstand: a pitcher of ice water, a clean glass, a bottle of aspirin and a box of extra-absorbent tissues. Nothing more he could do.

Getting the older boys into bed was a cinch. He'd forgone the bath, brush-your-teeth routine. Their teeth wouldn't rot overnight, and they were going to lose most of them, anyway. Tye and Miles were tired—sleepy tired and tired of hearing their younger brother wail.

Jamie, on the other hand, was beyond tired, and that made the two-year-old beyond difficult. Jamie, the fussy sleeper, had his own room. A white crib had its unused front panel down so the little tike could crawl out without toppling over. Smiling teddy bears danced on the wallpaper, a football-shaped toy box overflowed with things that bounced and made lots of noise. A small lamp rested on a sturdy white dresser, its teddy bear base as jovial as the wallpaper. An open bag of disposable training pants sat in the corner beside a padded, blue rocking chair.

Jamie, dressed in a red-and-white striped playsuit, reached into the bag and scattered several pairs. "Want Mommy."

Dakota eyed the boy's damp bottom and wondered how to go about changing him without inciting a tantrum. "Mommy doesn't feel well. She's sleeping."

The cherubic face scowled. "Want Mommy."

"Sorry, sport. You've got me instead."

Paper underwear went flying. "No want you."

Dakota blew an exhausted breath and fell into the rocker. He'd never imagined having children, his or anyone else's, yet here he was, doing a lousy job at being a father. Husband, too. His wife shunned his sexual advances, and his kids expected candy at every turn. Well, not tonight, he thought. He'd get through this without lollipops or cigarettes, he decided, shrugging off the craving.

"Get undressed, Jamie," he said, knowing the kid was capable of the task. The boy peeled off his clothes whenever the mood struck and ran around bare-butt naked at least once a week.

The child set his jaw in a gesture that reminded Dakota of Annie. "No want to. Want Mommy."

I want your mommy, too, he thought. "If I have to come over there and get you ready for bed, you're going to be sorry." It was an idle threat, but it sounded dadlike so he went with it.

The rug rat wrinkled his face and tossed a pair of the disposable training pants at Dakota's feet. "Daddy go 'way."

Daddy.

When Dakota's heart lunged to his throat, he nearly choked on it. Jamie had never called him Daddy before. He grinned. "If you don't behave, I'll sing to you."

The two-year-old twisted the underwear in his hands and scooted away. "Daddy sing bad. Go 'way."

Daddy.

His eyes were going to water any minute now. Spying one of the child's favorite stuffed animals in the toy box, he grabbed hold of it. If Jamie wasn't ready to cooperate with Daddy, maybe he'd respond to the ragged bear aptly named Teddy.

Dakota brought the worn blue face next to his own. If a bear could talk, what would it say? And how would its voice sound? Low and gruff? High and squeaky? Would it be a friend of Goldilocks? Eat porridge for breakfast?

Dakota glanced around the room. God, he felt stupid.

Teddy gave him an empty look, and he nearly tossed the animal back until he caught the need in Jamie's soulful brown eyes. The child had inched closer.

An animated voice, much different from Dakota's, said hello to the two-year-old at the same time that a blue paw reached out.

Jamie whispered a shy "Hi" and accepted the handshake.

"Are you ticklish?" the bear asked.

The child narrowed his shoulders as though anticipating what came next.

Teddy didn't disappoint. He jumped forward and ruffled Jamie's hair, gave Dakota's a swat, then nibbled on the boy's arm until he grinned and giggled.

The bear danced and sang but no one booed him offstage even though his singing voice could have doubled for a sick cow. He talked about nursery rhymes and holidays, Santa

Claus, the Easter Bunny and all of his favorite cartoon characters.

When Teddy handed Jamie a pair of the paper undies and asked him to get ready for bed, the child removed his playsuit and donned the dry trainers along with a pair of clean pajama bottoms. Much to the bear's surprise, he even tossed the soiled outfit into a nearby trash can. Teddy thanked the boy and decided to leave the jumpsuit right where it was, even if the hamper would have been his choice.

Teddy tossed back his head and made a loud, yawning noise. "Would it be okay if your daddy rocked us to sleep? I'm tired."

Jamie nodded and crawled onto his father's lap. Dakota stroked the child's cheek in amazement and tucked a silent blue bear against him.

"Daddy?"

"Hmm?"

"Pee-pee."

He chuckled. "Don't have to, sport, but thanks for asking."

Jamie knit his brows. "Pee-pee, Daddy. Me."

Dakota flew out of the rocker. They made it to the bathroom just in time, and when the deed was done the boy received a hearty hug and a high-five.

"Tell Mommy," Jamie squealed.

Persistent little begger. "We'll tell her tomorrow. Tonight we sleep."

"Lollipop?"

Oh, what the hell. He hoisted Jamie up and headed for the kitchen. Once the kid ate his candy and nodded off, he was slipping outside for a much-deserved smoke.

Six

___

Dakota picked up the phone. Annie was at work, and the kids were with Maria, the housekeeper he'd secretly hired. Maria had offered to take the boys to the park, giving him a chance to make this call.

"Hello?" Harold answered.

"Hi, it's Dakota."

"How are the children?" came Harold's quick reply.

"They're doing great. Jamie even calls me Daddy now."

He heard a smile in the older man's voice. "And how is Annie? Does she call you husband?"

Dakota frowned. He wasn't about to admit that he hadn't made love to his wife yet. "Annie just got over the flu, but she's fine. She went back to work today." He tugged his free hand through his hair. "The reason I called was that I wanted to discuss Excalibur with you."

"The bull?"

"Yeah. I plan on getting in touch with some of my old sponsors to see if they might be interested in hosting a special event. Me and Excalibur. A one-time deal."

Strange, Dakota thought, how the bull he'd wanted to conquer so badly had destroyed him. Excalibur had never afforded any cowboy that eight-second thrill, so on that summer day when he'd finally drawn that notorious bull, he'd been certain he would complete the ride and relish a personal and professional victory. But that hadn't happened. Excalibur had crushed him instead.

"So you're ready to go back to the rodeo?" Harold asked.

"I'm ready to face Excalibur," Dakota responded. Ready to combat the anxiety that came with reliving the accident over and over again in his mind—the fall, the pounding of hoofs, the sound of his own bones breaking, the pain, the numbness, the slow-motion panic that followed. "I need to erase it, start over. Walk away this time."

"I understand," the older man said.

But would Annie? Dakota wondered. He knew Annie thought he was incapable of getting back on a bull, but that wasn't the case. Physically he'd recovered; it was his emotions that hindered him.

Dakota blew a windy breath. Unless he could end that bull's six-year undefeated streak, he would always be remembered as the cowboy Excalibur had trampled. And that made him feel like a shamed warrior, a man defeated in battle. Dakota needed to retire with dignity. To him, Cowboy Up was more than just a trendy phrase printed on T-shirts. It represented a motto to live by. He couldn't let his anxiety hold him back.

"I haven't told Annie yet," he admitted. "I'm worried it might upset her because of her dad. She's had a hard time getting over how he died."

"Her father was an irresponsible man. The circumstances of his accident were different from yours."

"Yeah, I know."

"Tell her. She will be fine. She will understand."

Dakota shook his head. He wasn't so sure. He needed to convince Annie that he was a dedicated husband and father, before he revealed his plan, give her time to accept him. Admitting that he planned on riding Excalibur again wouldn't help win his wife's affection. It was his duty to make this marriage work, a Cheyenne commitment he now believed was his destiny, something Harold expected of him.

Miles hopped up and down, watching Annie lace up her shoes. "Where are we going?"

She shook her head and smiled. She had already answered the anxious five-year-old's question three times. "Your Uncle Kody says it's a surprise."

The child sat on the edge of his mother's bed and clicked his heels. Aside from the spiked hair, he looked like a mini-replica of Dakota. Miles had taken to Wranglers, cowboy boots and Western shirts since his new father's arrival.

"Can't you at least give me a hint?" the boy persisted.

Annie finished lacing both shoes and stood. "Sweetheart, he didn't tell me where we were going or what the surprise is."

"You could ask him. He's in the kitchen."

She knew where her husband was. He lingered over the newspaper with a strong cup of black coffee every morning. A short walk and a cigarette would follow. Dakota lived on what Mary called Cheyenne time—a pace as unhurried as the clouds that drifted across the vast Montana sky. "Asking him would spoil the surprise."

Miles fidgeted, and Annie sat at the vanity and applied a dab of perfume. She didn't favor any particular brand. Her moods changed too much to adhere to one fragrance.

She gave her hair one last fluff and checked her makeup. Lately she'd found herself fussing over her appearance. She knew the reason, although she hated to admit it. She wanted to look appealing for Dakota.

Today she'd chosen casual attire: khaki pants, a white T-shirt and brown leather shoes, an outfit her husband would view as play clothes. He seemed to like the variety of her wardrobe, especially her nightgowns.

What woman wouldn't want a man like Dakota to notice her? He wasn't just handsome, he was kind—a natural care-giver, bringing her soup and crackers while she was sick, look-ing after the children, keeping them busy with creative activities so she could rest. He had even helped the kids make her get well cards.

Miles moved closer. "Can we go now?"

She reached for his hand and smiled. Miles—her impatient little artist. The card he'd constructed consisted of rose petals and glitter, shining specks of silver he'd sprinkled all over the house. "Let's check with Uncle Kody and see if he's ready."

They found Dakota at his usual spot at the table, newspaper spread, coffee mug steaming. Lifting his head, he peered up through his glasses. He wore them whenever Tyler was around. The gesture warmed Annie's heart. Dakota was an incredible father, even if he found ways to cheat.

He watched the kids three days a week, and on those occasions managed to create new silver designs, feed the boys, run a vacuum, dust and mop. Odd, she decided, because he wasn't the tidiest person while in her presence, and although he cooked, he rarely rinsed a single plate, much less scrubbed the stove. Truthfully, she suspected foul play—possibly a cleaning woman or even a whole crew. Annie smiled. One of these days she intended to catch him and wipe that I-can-do-everything smirk off his gorgeous face. Lately he was too darn perfect.

"Are you ready, Uncle Kody?" Miles asked, bobbing up and down once again. "'Cause we are."

Dakota winked at Annie, then answered the boy's question. "I haven't finished my coffee, son, and your brothers are still eating breakfast."

Miles smacked his hand against his thigh, and Annie crossed her arms. "Where are the boys having their breakfast?" she asked. Certainly not in the kitchen, since Dakota's newspaper dominated the table.

"In the living room. They're watching cartoons."

She didn't allow the kids to eat in the living room, but apparently Dakota did. Annie shook her head. Naturally Dakota wouldn't worry about food spills and juice stains on the furniture, not when he could hire someone to clean it up.

Miles plopped himself down at the table and rattled his

dad's newspaper as though trying to hurry things along. Dakota sipped his coffee and continued reading.

Annie went to the living room and checked on the other two boys. Tyler and Jamie sat side by side on the floor, way too close to the TV, each with their own box of cereal. Tyler's breakfast made it into his mouth, but Jamie's honey-flavored circles were strewn all over the floor.

"Hi, Mommy," the two-year-old said with a loving grin.

Her heart warmed. "Hi, baby." The vacuum cleaner would take care of the cereal, but that smile would remain with her forever.

Tyler looked over, too. He appeared confident in his glasses now. Tye's classic Cheyenne cheekbones were well-defined, but the slim line of his nose and wave in his hair had come from his biological father, a man who had been as fair and blond as Annie. Tyler was a handsome child, tall for his age and sullen in a way that would eventually drive women crazy. The big, brooding type always did.

For a moment Annie just stood and stared, wondering what a child of hers and Dakota's would look like. Beautiful, she decided. A sweet, rosy-cheeked baby with Dakota's thick, dark hair and her amber-colored eyes.

Oh, my God. She took a step back. Where had that insane thought come from?

Why, Dakota, of course. Mr. Charming had preyed on her emotions with his perfect husband-and-father routine. Damn it. The last thing she needed was to fall for him.

She glanced over at Tyler and Jamie again, then closed her eyes, trying to dispel the image of that sweet little baby. Annie knew better than to daydream about things that could never be.

The moment they reached their destination, Annie knew what Dakota's gift to the boys would be. Puppy Haven was just that. A pet store specializing in puppies.

Annie and Dakota wandered through the store, watching their kids scan each glass cubicle for the pet of their dreams. Miles changed his mind every other minute, going from beagles to poodles, while Tyler hung back quietly. Jamie toddled along in his bib-overalls, calling every dog "puppy."

Annie had to admit, each little furry face she saw, she wanted to take home. Some barked through the glass, others pawed and wiggled.

"Do you want a puppy, Jamie?" Dakota asked.

The child nodded.

"Then pick out one you like."

Annie shook her head. Her husband certainly had an unorthodox method of choosing a dog. Just set the kids loose in a pet store. She would have preferred to buy a canine encyclopedia, choose several appropriate breeds, then evaluate the information. Telling a two-year-old to "pick out one you like" wouldn't have occurred to her.

When Jamie finally stopped and pressed his face to one of the glass cages, Dakota and Annie stood back and watched. The lone puppy, labeled a bulldog, waddled forward and pressed its nose to the glass as though mimicking the boy. Jamie giggled, and the pup panted. It had a flat, smashed face and dark, droopy eyes. Thick wrinkles rolled across its sturdy fawn and white body. It was ugly, Annie thought, in an adorable kind of way.

Dakota chuckled. "Somebody found a friend."

Annie scanned the dog's label. A nine-hundred-dollar friend.

Jamie looked back at his parents. "Mine," he said.

Dakota motioned to the salesman. "Can we see this dog?"

The young man returned a moment later with the bulldog in tow.

While Jamie hugged the stocky puppy, Annie bombarded the salesman with questions, learning this breed belonged to the mastiff family and were officially referred to as English bulldogs because they originally hailed from Great Britain. They were quiet and well mannered, she was told, affectionate and calm. Of course, all that perfection came with a hefty price tag.

Dakota grinned as the puppy nuzzled Jamie's cheek, its jowls rolling. "He's a tough-looking little guy, isn't he?"

"He'll follow your kid everywhere he goes," the salesman said. "These dogs are loyal. They look mean but they're not. Couldn't ask for a better pet."

"Mine," Jamie squealed again.

Annie reached down to pet the puppy, stunned by its downy fur. Because of the animal's bulky appearance, she had expected its coat to be coarse. "This dog is really expensive," she whispered to Dakota.

He shrugged. "I don't mind spending the dough. Look how happy Jamie is."

And that was the end of that. Her two-year-old had a nine-hundred-dollar dog. A dog that would eventually weigh fifty to seventy pounds and expect to sleep in the child's bed, no doubt.

Tyler and Miles praised their younger brother's puppy, then went on to search for their own.

Fifteen minutes later Miles surprised his family by choosing the smallest dog in the world. He wanted a Chihuahua. The tiny red pup, not nearly as costly as the bulldog, sat cupped in the five-year-old's hand, peering up at Annie through round, expressive eyes. Another adorable male, this one with ears almost as big as its entire body.

Miles decided to call the puppy Taco after his favorite TV dog. "But I might have to learn Spanish," the boy said, "so he'll understand me. Chihuahuas are from Mexico and their poop's not very big because they're so little."

Dakota and Annie laughed. Apparently Miles had been considering the clean-up factor involved in owning a canine.

Dakota turned to Tyler. "Didn't you find a dog, son?"

Tyler looked around uncomfortably, twisting the end of his T-shirt. "There's lots of nice dogs here but...well...I was thinking there's probably some orphaned dogs at the pound that need homes."

Annie's heart clenched. Sweet, sensitive Tyler.

Dakota swallowed as though fighting down a lump forming in his throat. "I think you're probably right. Soon as we're done here, we'll head over to the pound, okay?"

The eight-year-old smiled. "Okay."

They made it to the animal shelter by one o'clock. Miles carried an alert, little Taco while Dakota lugged around Jamie's twenty-pound puppy. On the ride over, the two-year-old kept calling the pup a bull*frog* instead of a Bull*dog,* so Annie had suggested they name him Jeremiah. Of course, the kids had never heard the song about Jeremiah the bullfrog and when she sang the lyrics, they laughed as though she'd made the song up. But since the dog in question had wagged its tail merrily, all agreed he liked the name.

Tyler walked along quietly, petting the dogs through the bars. When he stopped at one particular cage and studied a rather shy, scruffy mutt that stood behind an array of yapping hounds, Annie knew her son had found his best friend.

The medium-size black dog, a shepherd mix of some kind, sported pointed ears and a long snout. Hip bones protruded from its gaunt frame while patches of missing fur exposed chapped skin on its rump. Annie noticed the poor creature, another male, had a sweet disposition and an eager-to-please look in its gray eyes even if its appearance sorely lacked luster.

As the timid pooch inched closer, Dakota stroked its head while balancing Jeremiah in his arms. Jeremiah sniffed the newcomer, and Taco squeaked out a bark, reminding everyone of his tiny presence. "This is a fine dog," Dakota told Tyler. "We'll get him fit as a fiddle in no time."

"I'm going to call him Dog Soldier," the boy announced.

Annie stroked the top of Tyler's head. He had just paid his adoptive father a well-deserved honor. Dakota's great-great-grandfather was a Dog Soldier, the bravest of the Cheyenne warriors. Annie knew Dakota had inherited a bone-handled knife that had belonged to his ancestor and had used it in a private ceremony to make Jill his blood sister.

When Dakota smiled at Tyler, the eight-year-old grinned back at him. Annie watched their faces and realized a special bond had just been formed.

Later that evening, after the dog chaos had settled, Annie retreated to the sewing room with her sketch pad. Although engrossed in the details of a custom design, when Dakota entered the room, she found herself smiling. The scent of his freshly showered skin wafted to her nostrils, heightening her creative impulse to design a sensual garment.

He approached the drawing table, and she looked up. His slightly damp, towel-dried hair fell across his forehead, and a pair of drawstring sweats rode low on his hips. He wore no shirt, no shoes.

Dakota rolled his shoulders. "I made the kids a batch of popcorn, gave them a blanket and parked them in front of the TV with a Disney video."

"Which one?"

He grinned. "The one with all the dalmatians. I thought the dogs might enjoy that one, too."

She smiled again, this time with her heart. "You're a good dad, Dakota."

A proud beam brightened his dark eyes. "Thanks. It's getting easier. Jamie's really coming around."

Buttered popcorn in the living room was sure to make a mess, but she decided now wasn't the time to reprimand him about the house rules. The kids seemed to thrive on the freedom Dakota allotted, making her wonder if a compromise of rules was in order. And although she wouldn't have chosen lollipop rewards as a potty-training method, she had to admit it worked. Jamie had a lot fewer accidents.

Annie slid the pencil behind her ear and gazed up at Dakota again. His roping arena was nearly completed, so steers would be arriving soon. That miniranch was underway: dogs, horses, steers. Dakota had grown up around cowboy sports. His father, although retired now, had been a professional team roper. Dakota used to heel for his dad during practice runs, a father-son activity they had both enjoyed.

Reaching for her pencil, Annie wondered how Dakota could throw a rope these days when his back bothered him too much to sleep on a couch? Something didn't add up.

"Just how much roping do you plan to do?" she asked.

He cocked his head. "What brought that on?"

"Your arena is almost done, and I was thinking it seems

weird that you can ride and rope, but you can't sleep on the couch."

He pushed his damp hair off his forehead, then winced. "I guess I exaggerated a little."

Annie narrowed her eyes. "Exaggerated or lied?"

He shifted his bare feet. "Lied is a bit strong, don't you think?"

She shot him a pointed stare. *"Dakota."*

"Okay. I lied." He lowered his head and viewed her harsh expression. "Are you mad?"

A knot of irritation formed in her stomach. "Yes, I'm mad. That was a low-down trick to get into my bed."

He stepped back. "Does that mean you're banishing me to the living room?"

"I don't know." She'd come to enjoy his presence beside her at night, but the fact that she'd been conned didn't sit well. "Do you still have back problems or not?" Because if he did, the steers would have to go.

"Not really, no." A sheepish grin tilted his lips. "I walk a little funny, but I guess that doesn't count."

"You walk just fine." Somehow his apologetic smile managed to loosen the knot in her stomach. Dakota had suffered enough from the rodeo accident. He had lost his career over it, and chasing down a few steers wasn't nearly as dangerous as bull riding. He would never go back to that. He couldn't, she realized. That was the extreme of the cowboy sports, and, regardless of how well he'd healed, bull riding would surely threaten those old injuries.

"I suppose you can stay in the bedroom. After all, we did agree it would be best for the boys. But if you're keeping any other secrets—"

"I'm not," he interrupted, much too quickly.

His body language said otherwise. The kids shifted their feet when they weren't being completely honest. How did that saying go? *The only difference between men and boys is the price of their toys.*

This time Annie thought she knew his secrets. Not only did she suspect a housekeeper, she suspected he bribed the kids with candy to keep the cleaning lady a secret. Although the candy jar remained full, she noticed the contents periodically changed. She had bought one mixed variety, whereas Dakota had apparently bought another, trying to pass it off as the same. Being a mom for the past two years had alerted her to the signs of sneaky, kid-type deception. Dakota wasn't any better at trickery than the boys.

Annie pretended to study her drawing. Initially his secret keeping hadn't bothered her, but now she wondered if it could prove to be a problem. What if his next little white lie wasn't so innocent? Soon he'd be on the road selling his jewelry, living a free and temptation-filled life away from her and the kids. Her dad had taken advantage of his time away from home.

Annie frowned. Even though Dakota was no longer a rodeo star, he was still a handsome man, a magnet for buckle bunnies and the like.

He leaned over her shoulder and studied her sketch. "Why do you always make the girls so skinny?"

Aggravated by her own thoughts, she ignored his delicious scent. "Body proportions are longer in fashion illustration."

He made a face. "Looks weird to me."

Annie pushed a blank sheet of paper toward him. *Okay, Mr. Know-It-All, who can't even clean the house without help.* "I suppose you can do better?"

He grinned and grabbed her pencil. Ready for a break, Annie offered him the chair and stood back to watch, preparing to gloat. But surprisingly, what began to appear went beyond the amateurish rendering she had expected. Curious, she moved closer. Although he didn't follow a trained method of figure drawing, the curvaceous woman he created had a lifelike quality. Too lifelike in some areas.

Annie cleared her throat. "That's actually very good. But for starters, her breasts are too big."

He raised the sketch eye level. "No they're not."

"Models are rarely that busty." She decided not to mention the fact that his drawing had aroused nipples whereas hers did not.

Dakota turned his head and stared right at her bustline. "Yours are this big."

Annie resisted the urge to fling her arms across her chest. "I'm not a model." She still wore the same clothes from that morning. And although her T-shirt was far from revealing, she felt exposed. Her seamless, flesh-colored bra didn't offer much in the way of protection, especially since her nipples had decided to rise to the occasion.

He lifted his gaze. "How come?"

Annie didn't know what was worse. Having him stare at her breasts or having him stare directly into her eyes after he'd just stared at her breasts. "How come what?"

"How come you're not a model?"

Her mouth nearly dropped. What planet had he been living on? "Because I'm too short, not pretty enough, my breasts and hips are too big, and I'm at least five pounds heavier than I should be."

He pulled away and stared at her again. Really stared, much to her dismay. She probably should have left the overweight part off. He'd be looking for those extra pounds now, and she'd said five when seven or eight would have been more accurate.

"As far as I'm concerned, you're built the way a woman should be. And you're wrong about not being pretty enough."

No wonder he posed such a threat. Dakota could certainly charm when he chose to. "Thank you." A chill tingled her spine. His stare had turned downright ravenous.

Dakota bounced his knees. "Come here."

Annie nibbled her bottom lip. Undoubtedly *here* meant his lap. She allowed her gaze to roam over him. Men weren't supposed to be beautiful, yet this one looked as though he'd been sculpted by an angel and dipped in bronze. Beads of water dripped from the ends of his hair and onto his chest like glittering diamonds.

Without a second thought, she straddled his lap, discovered his aroused state, then withheld a giggle when he groaned. "Sorry."

Another rough sound escaped his throat as he grabbed hold

of her waist. "Do that again. Only this time without the apology."

With a surge of feminine power, she slipped her arms around his neck and rocked her hips. "What do you have on under those?"

"The sweats?" His fingers crept up her T-shirt. "Nothing, darlin'. What you feel is what you get."

What she *felt* was a man with healthy appetite, a sexual craving. Curious to sample what he offered, she leaned in and flicked her tongue across his neck. He tasted of soap, male flesh and desire. Wanting more, she followed a path with her tongue down the center of his chest, then gasped when his heartbeat thudded against her lips.

He fisted her hair, his fingers clawing her scalp. "There's a name for women like you."

Annie looked up. "Are you calling me a tease?"

"No, darlin'. I was thinking more along the lines of a wife."

Fascinated by the rough timbre of his voice, she licked the corner of his mouth, snaring his lips in a quick kiss. "So I'm acting like a wife, am I?"

Dakota ignited the playful kiss by bathing her bottom lip with his tongue. "Yeah, a good one."

"How good?"

"This good." He raised his hips, caught her bottom and ground his erection against the front of her trousers.

Hot, hard and hungry. *Good* no longer applied. Not when hands and mouths quested. His tongue pillaged and plundered while hers sipped and nursed.

Clutching handfuls of his hair, she watched hers spill over them like a pale blond curtain. Everything about them seemed so right together—the contrast of their skin, color of their eyes, contour of their bodies.

Could his heart leap into her chest? she wondered. For the beats had intensified into one rapid, thundering ache—two life forces pumping as one.

"I want you." He pressed his forehead to hers, his confession wavering on a plea. "So damn bad."

What he wanted, Annie realized, was heathen sex, naked

bodies climaxing in fury. She swallowed her next breath. She couldn't help but wonder how it would feel to have him inside her, moving rhythmically. She had fantasies, too. Dreams of an erotic honeymoon.

Dakota kissed her again, hard and deep, but the sound of children arguing and dogs barking stilled them both. Annie steadied herself as the room rotated around an imaginary axis, putting yet another spin on the uncharacteristic situation. Fantasizing about sex while her kids yelled and threw popcorn didn't seem possible. Yet here she was, doing just that, lusting over Dakota with a vengeance.

Willing herself to take control, she planted her feet firmly on the floor. "I think the kids are fighting over whose dog did what." Any minute now, she knew, Jamie would be wailing. "I better go settle this."

Dakota dragged his hand through his hair in apparent frustration, then moaned piteously when her body left his. "I'd go with you, but—" he motioned toward his lap, "—I'm not exactly presentable."

She stole a glance and felt her nipples tingle. "You better start wearing briefs under your sweats, cowboy."

"Yeah." A grin slashed across his face. "And you better kiss me senseless more often."

Senseless, Annie thought, had described her behavior to a T. And although she knew better, she couldn't seem to stop herself. She wanted her husband in the worst way.

Seven

Eager to be with his wife, Dakota entered their bedroom. Two hours had passed since their flirtation, and he wanted more. He wanted to kiss her again, hold her body next to his and feel her quiver.

"Hi, Daddy."

Dakota jerked his head up. The tiny voice had come from the bed.

Immediately Jamie's smile chased his heart and tagged it. The boy lay nestled in Annie's arms, his cherubic face beaming. *He's our flesh and blood now,* Dakota thought. *Mine and hers.*

"Hi," Dakota repeated the greeting.

Seeing Annie with that dark little head pressed against her bosom did strange things to him inside. Awe and pride, he decided, a new emotion where Annie was concerned. Dakota squinted to mask a frown. Wife or not, he wasn't sure if he liked feeling sappy over a woman. With the kids it was different. He had accepted them as a part of himself long ago, even though he had never envisioned raising them. Just as he'd never envisioned Annie as his wife, at least, not before Harold had approached him about marrying her.

Dakota stood, his bare feet riveted to the carpet. He had imagined Annie in bed plenty of times, but not with a two-year-old tucked into a cozy ball beside her. His fantasies had never bordered on paternal. He was used to thinking of her as his wild, platinum-haired fantasy, but with her arms wrapped around their son, that wasn't easy to do. The boy's adoration conjured sweet, wholesome images that made his heart feel kind of soft. He squinted again, hoping his frown wasn't overly apparent. This marriage thing wasn't supposed to make a romantic fool out of him. Duty and honor was one thing, but melting like a clump of wax was another. No, he didn't appreciate this syrupy sensation one bit. Sure, he wanted to be a good husband, but to him that meant denoting strength and masculine character. Warriors didn't melt over their women. A husband was a protector, a provider, a sexual partner.

And that's what he'd been hoping for tonight. Foreplay. Some hot and heavy groping. "Jamie, do you want Daddy to carry you to your crib?" he asked.

"No." The child shook his head vigorously. "Me and J-miah sleep here."

At the sound of his mispronounced name, Jeremiah the bull-dog poked his head out from beneath the blanket and gazed up at Dakota through droopy eyes and an enormous yawn.

Putting his sexual frustration aside, Dakota smiled. The trio in bed was about as cute as they came. The woman wore a pale-pink nightgown, the child, baby-blue pajamas. Her arms were long and slender, the boy's chubby and dimpled. "Annie, what's going on?"

She stroked the child's hair. "Jamie couldn't sleep in his own room because the puppy kept whining. And the crib's too narrow for both of them. Besides, the dog could get hurt if he tried to jump out. Our bed seemed like the only solution to a good night's sleep."

Dakota moved forward. That sappy feeling had come back, but he couldn't seem to stop it. He wouldn't trade the grin on Jamie's face or the tender look in Annie's eyes for anything.

Just this once, he'd allow himself to feel warm and fuzzy and stupid inside.

Just this once, he reiterated, because the last thing he wanted was to stumble around thinking about his wife all the time. Hadn't he spent enough years with her on his mind? This marriage was supposed to take care of that obsession. He studied the column of Annie's neck, the length of her hair. It would, he realized, once they made love. Sex was the cure. Of course, not tonight. Tonight he would fulfill his role as a father.

Dakota turned the three-way lamp down, rather than off. He knew Jamie still slept with a nightlight. "Is there room in there for me?"

Jamie waved his arms then patted the bed, apparently thrilled to have both parents at his beck and call. "Here, Daddy." The boy directed his father to an empty space beside him and giggled as Dakota scooted in.

"Me and J-miah sleep here every night."

That won't do much for the love life, Dakota thought. "No, son. We'll buy you and Jeremiah your own bed."

The child wiggled between his parents, squeaking the mattress springs. "No more crib?"

"That's right, no more crib."

He turned to his mother. "Me big boy, Mommy."

"I know, sweetheart." She stroked his cheek. "You're growing up so fast."

Silence settled over them like a warm, summer breeze. Annie rocked Jamie in the crook of her arm while Dakota, wanting to be a part of the physical contact, touched the top of the boy's head. The dog, not to be outdone, nuzzled the child's limp hand.

Annie whispered as Jamie drifted off to sleep. "Right after their parents died, Tyler and Miles would cuddle up with me. Sometimes we'd cry ourselves to sleep. Other times we talked about all the angels in Heaven."

Dakota watched the boy's lashes flutter against his cheeks. This little angel was earthbound. "I'm sorry I wasn't there for you, for the kids."

Annie turned her face toward his. "You were hurt. You

couldn't help it.'' She skimmed her finger from Jamie's cheek to Dakota's then back again. ''I used to cry for you, too. And pray. Who would have guessed that you'd be hospitalized in the same month that Jill died. It was such an awful time.''

An ache as big as Texas flooded his chest. She had cried for him? ''Still, I wish I could have been there. You shouldn't have had to grieve alone.''

''It's okay.'' Annie shifted the sleeping child so she could rest her head against her husband's shoulder. ''You're here now.''

Yeah, he was there now, feeling too damn emotional about her. Maybe he just needed to quit stalling and get back on the road. Dakota was and always would be a gypsy at heart. And with that in mind, he'd come up with a business venture that would give him purpose to be on the road, more than just selling his jewelry designs. Although he still hadn't heard from his sponsors about Excalibur, he knew it would be a one-time event. After that, he would still need a career of some kind.

Besides, Annie would probably be glad to have some time to herself. Dakota knew he'd disrupted the order in which she lived. She followed rules, made lists, believed in organization, whereas he blew along like a tumbleweed, leaving cigarette butts in his wake.

He would wait just a little while longer, he decided, because soon they'd be lovers. With each kiss they shared, he could feel her resistance soften and drift away. He toyed with a lock of Annie's hair. Yeah, he'd wait. He didn't want to sleep alone in some motel room without knowing how it felt to be inside her.

''Annie?''

''Hmm?''

''Do you want to go out this weekend? Just the two of us? You know, sort of like a date?''

She snuggled a little closer, bringing Jamie with her. ''Sure. I think I'd like that. I haven't been on a date in ages.''

Dakota found himself smiling. He'd buy his wife a nice dinner, then take her to a remote spot to neck. And he knew just the spot, since he'd already checked out the area. Making out in a pickup used to be one of his favorite pastimes. His smile curved into a full-blown grin. It seemed some things never changed.

"Do you remember the first time we saw each other again, you know, after that last summer you spent with my family?"

She looked up at him. "Sure. Mary, Jill and I were starting college, and we'd just moved into our first apartment. You were in between rodeos so you stayed with us for a couple of days."

Four days to be exact, and even now, he recalled that reunion vividly. He'd walked into their apartment, hugged Mary and Jill, then stopped dead in his tracks. There stood Annie, all grown-up, silky hair spilling over her shoulders, breasts high and full, hips round and womanly. His fantasy girl come to life. "Did you know that I'd thought you were the most gorgeous creature I'd ever seen? That I'd considered asking you out?"

"Are you kidding? You were the gorgeous one, Dakota. Even though I had just turned eighteen, I felt like a knobby-kneed adolescent all over again. I remember Mary kept asking me why I was acting so strange."

He kissed the top of her head and drew the blanket tighter around their son. "Maybe we should have gotten together back then." Because maybe if they'd become lovers early on, she wouldn't have gone off and gotten herself engaged.

"I don't think we would have made a very good pair. I wouldn't have handled your profession very well."

Hating the jealousy nipping his gut, he scowled. "Of course you handled football players just fine."

She stiffened in his arms. "That's not fair to bring Richard into this, Dakota. He wasn't a professional football player. Besides, football players don't get killed on the field."

Dakota knit his brows. His profession always came down to her dad. "Your father shouldn't have died, Annie. He shouldn't have ridden that day." Rumor had it that Clay Winters had been hung over from a drunken binge the night before, his reflexes slow and sloppy. When he'd fallen from the bull and crawled to his feet, he couldn't move quickly enough. The animal had charged him in one lethal blow.

She kept her voice low, even though it sounded strained. "I know how much my dad was drinking then. The divorce had just been finalized, and he wasn't handling it well. But other cowboys have been killed, too. Men who were in control of their senses. Bull riding isn't safe. I've never understood it.''

"It's who I am," Dakota responded, feeling the need to defend the only life-style he'd ever known.

"It's who you *were*," she countered, "not who you are now." When he flexed his fingers, she brushed the top of his hand with a gentle touch. "I used to worry about you all those years, as it was. Being emotionally involved would have made it that much harder. I'm truly sorry that your career ended in such a tragic way, but I'm glad that part of your life is over. I'm not cut out to be a bull rider's wife.''

He squeezed her hand, uncertain of what to say. As he closed his eyes, he knew sleep would be a long time coming.

When morning arrived, streams of light peered through the curtains. Dakota squinted and gazed around. Noticing he was alone and the ringing he'd heard was the phone and not the alarm clock, he leaped across the bed and lunged for the receiver.

"Hello?''

A Texas twang drawled his name. "Dakota?''

"Yeah.''

"Hey, you sound sleepy. I didn't catch you at an inconvenient time, did I? Heard you married some gorgeous blonde.''

Dakota laughed. The man on the other end of the line had to be Billy Moreau, the marketing director for Outlaw Boots and one of his former sponsors. "You got news for me, Billy?''

"You always did cut to the chase." Billy cleared his throat. "Are you ready to ride that bull, I mean really ride him and not get dumped on your ass? 'Cause if you are, we've got a deal for you.''

Dakota snapped to attention, his groggy voice suddenly sharp and alert. "I'm listening.''

"We're talking big bucks here, but you've got to make a qualified ride. You won't get paid for landing on your butt, regardless of how cute the female population thinks it is.''

Dakota chuckled. "I'll ride that bull and when I do you'll be eating those words, Texas boy, along with that big ol' Stetson you wear."

Billy exaggerated his drawl. "Fair enough. But that's not the end of it. Just to sweeten the pot, we'll throw in an easy endorsement. You know, look good in our boots and pose for some pictures like you used to."

"And I'll get paid for the endorsement even if I fall on this cute butt of mine, right?" Not that he planned on letting that happen. He'd ride Excalibur this time. No getting bucked off, no wrecks. He had to succeed. His emotional well-being depended on it. He couldn't live with the anxiety anymore, the fear of never letting it go, of seeing himself paralyzed over and over again.

"Yes, sir. Once the public finds out you're ballsy enough to climb back on that bull, your face is going to sell us some boots." Billy cleared his throat again. "You ready to talk numbers now?"

An hour later Dakota's call ended. He sat at the rolltop desk, his heart thumping wildly. Outlaw had offered him quite a deal. And although the money involved wasn't his motivating factor, it would be enough to get his business venture off the ground with plenty to spare.

As Dakota reached for his jeans, he recalled Annie's words from the previous night. *I'm not cut out to be a bull rider's wife.* Well, she didn't have a choice, he decided. He had to do this.

Annie had warned him about keeping secrets, but this couldn't be helped. He needed to face that bull just as much as he needed his wife to become his lover. Unfortunately, keeping quiet was the only way to have both.

Mary stood behind Annie, gazing at her reflection in the vanity mirror. "Wow, you look great."

"Thank you." Annie drew a deep breath. The black dress she'd chosen cinched at the waist and flared at the hip, complementing the hourglass figure she'd always detested. Dakota's appreciation of her rounded curves made her a little bolder, though. The deeply scooped, button-front dress re-vealed a hint of cleavage, and her sexiest silk lingerie was in place, including a black garter belt and lace-top stockings, just in case he asked or tried to sneak a peek.

Annie added a touch of rose-tinted blush to her cheeks, thinking she needed a bit more color. Sometimes she thought her platinum hair drained her skin, other times she thought it was her best asset. Tonight she wore it loose, since the pale strands made a striking contrast against the ebony dress. Turn-ing on the vanity stool, she caught Mary's eye. "Can you believe I'm nervous?"

"About going out with my brother? You're married to the guy. What's there to be nervous about?"

"Tonight feels different." Because she felt different. Be-cause she had decided she would make love with him. Not tonight, of course, but soon. She couldn't deny her hunger much longer, and she needed to get Dakota out of her system.

Mary sat on the edge of the bed and flashed a comical grin. "Remember when we were kids and he made me mad, I used to tell his girlfriends what a jerk he was."

Annie couldn't help but laugh. "They never believed you."

"No. He's always had an easy time getting girls." Mary fingered the quilt. "Except for now."

"I'm the exception."

"Yes, you are."

Annie slipped on a pair of stiletto pumps, then tugged at the hem of her dress, wondering if it was too short. It rode several inches above the knee. "I've decided to give in," she said with a slight scowl.

The brunette tossed her braid over her shoulder. "So why are you frowning? Being sexually attracted to your husband isn't a bad thing."

"I'm a twenty-eight-year-old virgin. I'm not used to think-ing of sex as a recreational sport." Anxious, she dug through her jewelry box and retrieved two different earrings. Holding one style to each ear, she questioned her friend. "Which pair?" Dakota had made both.

Mary pointed to the dangling silver feather by her left ear. "The other ones are too little, they don't show up as well."

Feeling like a teenager getting ready for her first date, Annie fumbled with the feather earrings then glanced down at her feet. "Should I wear Western boots instead?"

"I don't know. Put them on and let's see how they look."

She dug through the closet and hauled out the Outlaw box. The lizard-skin boots felt like slippers compared to the skinny-heeled pumps. "What do you think?"

"Wear those. They look cute with that dress. And if I know Dakota, he'll probably want to take you to a cowboy bar. Old habits die hard."

Some of her husband's old habits were her biggest concern. "I guess I'm ready."

Mary drew her knees up. "You can say it, Annie."

"Say what?"

"That you're in love with him."

"I am not!" She glared at her friend. "Just because I'm willing to sleep with him doesn't mean I've fallen for him." How could Mary accuse her of being in love with Dakota? These days, Annie knew how to protect her heart. "He's an attractive man, and I don't want to be a virgin for the rest of my life. It's as simple as that."

She sat on the vanity stool again, only this time with her back to the mirror. The other woman appeared to be studying her gestures. Uncomfortable about the topic of conversation, Annie wrung her hands, resisting the urge to pop up and search the jewelry box for a bracelet to wear.

"Why does falling in love with Dakota worry you so much? You're married with three small children. It's the ideal situation, considering the circumstances."

"Damn it, Mary, I'm not in love with him." She would never let that happen. Dakota wasn't about to stick around. This conventional life would bore him soon enough, and she didn't intend to be left brokenhearted. She had learned her lesson with Richard. Annie preferred to keep a clear head where Dakota was concerned. They would become lovers, then part ways when the time was right. No expectations other than devotion to their children. "And he's not going to fall in love with me, either. He married me so I could keep the kids."

"I think you're wrong." Mary met her gaze. "I think he's confused by his feelings, so he's fighting it. He's wanted you for years."

"He's wanted to sleep with me. That's not exactly a lifetime commitment."

"True, but ten years is a bit long to be lusting after someone. I think it's more than just sex. He's probably half in love with you already, he just hasn't figured it out yet."

Was that the sister or the psychologist talking? Annie wondered. The sister, she decided hastily. Dakota didn't act like a man on the verge of falling in love. He seemed too casual about their relationship and much too eager to get back on the road. And ten years of lust wasn't so unusual. For some men the chase proved as thrilling as the conquest.

"Dakota's a great father," Annie offered in his defense. "I know he loves the kids."

"He's crazy about you, too." When Annie shook her head, Mary continued in a determined voice. "You know darn well my parents let him run wild, buying into that boys-will-be-boys excuse. They never even reprimanded him for sleeping around." She sighed, clearly displeased with her brother's rearing. "The only thing they stressed was that he practice safe sex. Dakota wasn't groomed for falling in love. No one expected it of him, so he doesn't expect it, either."

Nice try, Mary. I know you mean well, but you're wrong. You want your big brother to change, but that isn't going to happen. He is what he is.

"I don't think we have time for this conversation. Dakota's probably wondering what's taking me so long." Annie didn't imagine him pacing the living room floor, though. Dakota Graywolf wouldn't pace over a woman.

"One look at you and he'll decide you were worth the wait."

"Thanks." Annie grabbed an evening bag and stuffed her license, a tube of lipstick and a compact into it. "You're a good friend. I know you want what you think is best for me." *But my husband isn't the answer. He won't be mine forever.*

Eight

Just as Mary had predicted, Dakota took Annie to a local cowboy bar. They had eaten dinner at a five-star restaurant and now they entered The Horseshoe holding hands.

Annie gazed around. Aside from the Western attire of the patrons, it wasn't all that different from other clubs. A band played recognizable cover tunes as partners danced and cocktail waitresses squeezed through the crowd.

Dakota snagged a corner table just as another couple departed. Grateful, Annie took the chair her husband offered. Standing in a crowded bar wasn't her cup of tea. At least the table provided a small measure of comfort and privacy.

When their waitress arrived, a perky girl with big hair and a smile to match, Dakota ordered a bottle of Mexican beer, and Annie chose a glass of zinfandel. Dakota seemed completely at ease, at home, so to speak. But not Annie. She had always avoided cowboy bars. Her dad had spent too much time in them, dancing, drinking, chasing women.

Strange, she thought, how Dakota's dad had befriended her

father. Clay Winters and Tucker Graywolf didn't have much in common but the rodeo. Tucker was dedicated to his family, a man actively involved in his children's lives. He might have catered to Dakota's whims, allowing the young cowboy too much freedom, but at least he openly loved his son.

"What are you thinking about?" Dakota asked.

"Our dads," she answered honestly.

"What about them?"

She shrugged. "How unlikely their friendship was, I guess."

Dakota looked up as their waitress brought their drinks. He thanked the bouncy brunette, paid with a large bill and left a sizable tip. When the girl was gone, he turned back to Annie. "You were part of that friendship, you know. My dad used to feel bad for you, trailing around the rodeo like a lost puppy. That's why he brought Mary to meet you."

Annie *had* felt like a lost puppy then. She had spent summer vacations with her dad, hating every minute of the rodeos he'd dragged her to. Mary and Jill had been her salvation. Dakota, too, she supposed. Her crush on him had kept her mind off her parents' volatile relationship, their on-again, off-again marriage.

Dakota jammed the lime wedge into his beer. "I know your dad had some problems, but he was proud of you. He used to call you his little princess."

She picked up her wine. "Let's change the subject, okay? I've spent too many years dwelling on the past." Thank goodness, she thought, the rodeo was out of her life for good. Dakota's retirement had severed the last tie, the pain and the memories.

"Sure, okay." He removed his cigarettes, looked around with a scowl, then slipped them back into his pocket.

Annie appreciated the smoking ban in restaurants and bars. Dakota, it appeared, did not. In her estimation, her husband smoked at least a pack a day.

"What do you think of the band?" he asked.

Although the song was familiar, she preferred soft rock to country, but decided not to mention that. "They're good."

"Yeah, this is a pretty nice place."

It was, she realized. It didn't fall into the rowdy, honky-tonk category.

He leaned forward. "There's something I'd like to tell you, but I don't want you to get mad."

She toyed with the stem of her glass, her curiosity piqued. "What? That the only reason you were going to ask me out ten years ago was to get me into bed?"

His expression turned sheepish. "No. I mean, sure, that was probably my main objective at the time, but that's not what this is about." After swallowing another swig of beer, he tapped on the bottle. "I kind of well, fudged about something lately."

Fudged? "You mean lied?"

"I had good reason."

Annie met his gaze, her stomach clenching. She didn't believe in good reasons to lie. "Go ahead."

"I haven't been the one cleaning our house."

He winced and she resisted the urge to laugh. The man looked positively tortured. It was all she could do not to leap across the table and hug him breathless. "So, who do I have to thank for taking care of the place?"

"A lady named Maria. The boys really like her, and she's even teaching Miles a little Spanish so he can communicate with Taco."

The laugh escaped. "Do you really think that Chihuahua will understand Spanish any better than English?"

His mouth stretched into a slow smile. "The little guy is from Mexico. God, you don't know how glad I am that you're not mad. I only kept it from you because I was embarrassed that I acted like such a big shot at the airport, bragging about how easy taking care of the boys would be. I had no idea how much of a mess three pint-size kids could make."

She decided not tell him that she'd already suspected the housekeeper and had intended to catch him red-handed. Right now she wanted to express the sentiment in her heart. "Thank you. Your honesty means a lot to me, Dakota."

A shadow hooded his eyes, and for a moment she wondered

if he still had other secrets. The thought faded as he reached for her hand and brushed his lips over her knuckles.

"You're beautiful, Annie."

"Thank you." He was the beautiful one, she thought. He made a striking figure in a turquoise and tan shirt, a light-brown hat dipped over his eyes. Dakota had an impressive collection of vintage shirts, early designs he paired with jeans and boots. His interest in fashion pleased her.

"I want to kiss you," he said, immediately tripping her pulse. "We haven't kissed nearly enough."

"Here?" She gazed around at the crowed bar. "You want to kiss here?"

He smiled. "We could dance."

And embrace on the dance floor, she supposed. A shiver climbed up her spine. "Okay."

He stood and extended his hand. Annie accepted it, her heart fluttering at the thought of being pressed against every gorgeous, denim-clad inch. The music was slow, the beat soft and easy.

He held her close as they swayed, the brim of his hat creating a private shield. Annie fitted her head against his shoulder and enjoyed the feel of his arm around her waist. The dance floor overflowed with other couples, but she hardly noticed. Suddenly there was only one tall man, one strong body.

Lifting her chin to look up at him, Annie skimmed her fingertips across his cheek. Dakota caught her hand, held it against his face, then lowered his mouth to hers. The kiss sent a flood of warmth coursing through her veins. The exchange was too deep for a public display, but Annie refused to care. She met his tongue with the same voracious need, knowing the rhythm they exhibited bordered on sexual.

When the kiss ended, Dakota pressed his mouth close to her ear. "I've wanted you for so long."

"I know," she whispered back, blocking out Mary's opinion of love. This was lust, pure and simple.

He caressed the small of her back, and she initiated the kiss this time, moved her body against his and captured his tongue.

They tasted and touched and sighed into each other's mouths until the song changed to an up-tempo beat.

Dakota took her hand. "Let's get out of here."

"And go where?" she asked.

He flashed a wickedly boyish grin. "Just come with me and find out."

As they traveled up a narrow road, Annie peered out the window at the ranches rolling by. It was exciting, she thought, to be with him, this man with the dark liquid eyes. Tonight he made her feel alive and just a little reckless. Kissing in public wasn't her style, but she'd enjoyed every moment of their flirtation.

When Dakota stopped the truck and killed the engine, Annie gazed out the windshield.

"This is beautiful." They sat atop a hillside overlooking acres of lush greenery and ripe vineyards. City lights winked in the distance like a painted backdrop while the sky hosted a sea of twinkling stars. "How did you find this place?"

Dakota unbuckled his seat belt and reached over to touch her hair. "I asked that teenage kid who delivers our hay if he knew of a quiet spot to take a girl."

Annie covered her mouth and sputtered in laughter. "You actually asked him something like that? That sweet-looking boy?"

Dakota rolled his eyes. "That kid's not as innocent as he looks. He bums a smoke off me every chance he gets. I figured he owed me this one." He elbowed her rib. "And quit giggling. We're supposed to be making out."

She elbowed him right back, and they both laughed. "We're a little old to be messing around in a car, don't you think?"

"This is a truck."

"Same thing."

"Not to me." He flashed what she considered his signature grin. The grin of a rabble-rouser, a rake. "You see, I lost my virginity in a truck, not a car. Big difference."

Annie quit giggling. "How old were you?"

"Oh, no." Dakota waved his hand. "We're not getting into specifics, here."

Yes we are, she decided. "Was she your girlfriend?"

He turned the key and lowered the windows as though he suddenly needed air. "I never should have brought it up."

"But you did, so it's too late to back out now." Annie scooted a little closer. Dakota rarely offered personal information. "So how old were you?"

He removed his hat, tossed it behind the seat, then ran his hands through his hair. She waited while he debated the issue by packing his cigarettes several times, pushing in the lighter, igniting one and inhaling as though his life depended on it. "I wasn't quite old enough to drive."

All that time and that's all he had to say? "Then whose truck was it?"

He took another drag. "Hers. She was older. You know, more experienced than me. And she wasn't my girlfriend. It was just a one-time thing."

"How much older was she?"

He shrugged. "Three or four years, I guess."

"Was she a blonde?"

Dakota blew a stream of smoke out the window. "You ask the damnedest questions."

"Well, was she?" Annie wanted to know where his blonde obsession had come from.

"No." He flicked the ashes. "She was a girl from the rez. Cheyenne, same as me. And just for the record, it was her idea."

"So you didn't enjoy it?"

He laughed a little. "I didn't say that. Now enough with the questions, okay?" He smashed the cigarette into the ashtray and snapped it shut. "And don't be offering information about your first time, because I don't want to know."

Even though she had nothing to tell, his admission made her curious. "Why not?"

Dakota reached for her hair again, slid his fingers through it. "Your hair looks silver in the moonlight. God, it's so pretty."

She poked a finger into his stomach. "You're avoiding my question."

He made a face. "You're too persistent, Annie. It's annoying."

"Dakota, answer my question."

"All right." He released her hair and watched it flow through his fingers. "I don't like thinking about you being with another guy, so I'd rather pretend there weren't any."

Suddenly she ached to touch him, cuddle in his arms and caress his face, trace the scar that interrupted his eyebrow. "There's something I need to tell you."

"No, don't." He pressed his finger to her lips. "Tonight there's only us. You and me and the moon and the stars. Ex-lovers aren't invited."

She kissed his finger. "This is important."

He closed his eyes as though her next words would hurt. She smiled and moved closer, nibbling and kissing his finger until he opened his eyes and watched. When she closed her mouth over it, his curious stare turned glassy.

As though caught between pleasure and pain, he pulled his hand away. "Just say it, Annie. Because if you have to seduce me in order to get it out, it must be bad."

She touched his eyebrow, traced the scar, then ran her fingertips over the sharp contour of his cheekbone. "You'll be my first."

A stunned expression froze his features right before a quick smile caught his lips. "Your first? As in *lover?*"

She nodded and brought his hand to her heart so he could feel the rapid beat. "Yes, as in *lover.*"

He held her heart and kissed her, long and slow, exploring her thoroughly. Tongues collided and teeth scraped, but she wanted more, more of him. More of everything. He tasted of spearmint, tobacco and the imported beer he'd drunk with dinner—a flavor as untamed and passionate as the man.

"Do you realize that you've just agreed to be my lover?" he asked, his voice low and aroused.

"You said it would happen."

"Yeah, but you never agreed before, never really gave me

permission." Reaching for the top button on her dress, he released it. "Do you know that I think about you every night? That I listen to you breathe and fantasize about touching you?"

She shivered as he toyed with the trace of fabric covering her breasts. "I've done that, too."

He took her hand and placed it against his fly. "Then touch me while I kiss you."

As Annie stroked him through his jeans, a forbidden pleasure chased chills up her spine. They were married, yet what they did seemed taboo. Maybe it was being parked on a hilltop, she mused, groping each other like teenagers.

Dakota unhooked her bra and lowered his mouth as the garment slid from her shoulders. He moved his lips in reverence, exploring her texture, her scent, the fullness of her breasts. She watched him lick and suckle, knowing the catlike purrs filling the night were her own. Beautiful, wild Dakota, she thought with a sigh. Moonlight danced in his eyes and sent sapphire streaks across his hair. With each pull of his mouth, she arched and gripped him tighter, urging him to throb as she did.

Desire roared in her ears and pounded in her blood, but if she unzipped his jeans as she longed to, there would be no turning back. "We shouldn't be doing this. Not now. I don't want to lose my virginity in a car."

"It's a truck," he reminded her. "And I wouldn't take you here."

"You would if I told you what I was thinking about doing."

He raised his head, his grin wicked. "Go ahead. Indulge me."

Annie felt herself blush. "Okay, but you have to promise that you won't try anything with me tonight. I don't want to make love for the first time when the kids are home. Besides that, your sister will be sleeping on the couch. I want us to have the house to ourselves when it happens."

"I promise. I can wait. Now just whisper it in my ear."

She took a deep breath then leaned forward, wondering how to word such a thing. In a shaky voice, she pressed her lips to his ear and described an act that involved her mouth and his anatomy.

He released what sounded like a cross between a painful laugh and a choking cough. "I can't believe you said that."

Annie hooked her bra and adjusted her dress. "You told me to tell you."

"I know, but now that's all I'm going to think about." He plowed all ten fingers through his hair, then pushed the power buttons excessively, apparently unaware that the windows were still open. "Is it hot in here?"

She withheld a smile. He looked about ready to jump out of his skin. "I think it's just you."

"Yeah, I guess so." He fumbled with the ignition key. "I think we'd better go home."

"Why?"

He backed the truck up and kicked it into gear. "Because I need a cold shower."

She slanted him a sideways glance and they both erupted into laughter. As the truck sped down the hill, Annie took her husband's hand. No, she didn't love Dakota Graywolf, but she liked him—a whole lot.

Annie and Dakota stood on the front porch. With a cool, 2:00 a.m. breeze rustling their clothes, they grinned like mischievous teenagers breaking curfew.

She leaned into him, then stumbled a little, drunk on his taste. "We better go inside before we start making out again." Despite Dakota's claim for needing a cold shower, they had kissed and groped in the driveway for the past hour, making each other warm and lusty eyed.

"I suppose you're right." He unlocked the door and ushered Annie inside.

Luckily a brass floor lamp had been left on. Annie didn't want to stumble again. Mary slept on the couch in a blanket bundle, her hair strewn across her face.

Dakota stared down at his sister. "Hey, Mary." After tossing his hat onto the coffee table, he shook her shoulder.

Annie widened her eyes. "What are you doing?"

"Waking her up."

"It's after two. She's not going to drive home now."

"I know." He shook Mary's shoulder again, more aggressively this time.

Peeking through her hair, the other woman roused. She blinked in rapid succession. "What...time...is it?"

"It's morning," Dakota answered.

Groggily Mary sat and peered through the blinds. "It's still dark out."

Annie placed her purse next to Dakota's Stetson. What reason did he have for disturbing Mary? Annie knew firsthand the other woman was a slow, if not cranky waker. They'd been roommates all through college. She and Jill used to joke about Mary's morning growl. *Give her a cup of coffee, quick,* Jill used to say, *either that or find me a whip and a chair.*

Annie glanced back at the kitchen, wondering if she should brew a fresh pot of coffee. Dakota didn't appear the least bit sensitive about Mary's awakening. He raised his voice while she closed her eyes and tugged the blanket around her.

"Don't you dare go back to sleep. I need to talk to you."

She squinted a dark stare. "This better be an emergency."

"It is." He sat beside her. "We need you to baby-sit next weekend. But I want you to take the kids to your house overnight."

Annie shifted her feet. Dakota had awakened his sister for that? A spiral of nervous excitement spun through her body. Apparently he wanted to secure their lovemaking date.

Mary pushed irritably at his shoulder. "This couldn't have waited until a reasonable hour?"

"No. I wouldn't have been able to sleep."

"What's so special about next weekend?"

He caught Annie's eye, then turned back to Mary. "I want some time alone with my wife. So can you baby-sit or not?"

A smile appeared on the psychologist's lips, but it faded as quickly as it had come on. "I'm sorry, but I have a workshop next weekend. I'll be out of town."

Dakota plowed his hand through his hair and cursed. "Can't you reschedule it or something?"

"Reschedule it?" His sister laughed. "There are several

hundred people attending. They're not going to make an exception for me.''

He cursed again. "Then don't go. We don't have anyone else to watch the kids overnight. Their regular baby-sitter isn't available for weekends anymore.''

Mary laughed again. "Jeez, Dakota. Calm down. I can take them the following weekend.''

He looked up at Annie, a frown furrowing his brow. "That's fifteen days away.''

Annie stepped forward. "That's fine.'' She reached for her purse. "Thank you, Mary. I'm sorry we woke you.'' She held her hand out to Dakota. "Come on, let's go to bed and let your sister get some sleep.''

He grumbled all the way to their room. "I'll bet she's going to one of those dumb acting workshops. What a waste of time.''

Annie closed the door, then flipped on the light. Mary still dabbled in the arts. It was she who had introduced Annie to all the classic movie greats, the celluloid heroes that reminded her of Dakota. "We'll survive.''

"Maybe you will.''

His mouth crushed hers as his hands wandered. She closed her eyes. The light suddenly seemed too bright. It added heat and his touch scorched her as it was. He feasted on her tongue with animalistic fury, clutched handfuls of her dress and tugged.

When she was good and dizzy and her dress askew, he stepped back. "Fifteen days.'' His groan expressed his pain. "Somehow, I've got to get through this.''

She pulled the hem of her dress down. He had raised it just enough that the top of her hose had been exposed. Now his wild-eyed look made her feel vulnerable. A bit like a virgin sacrifice. "Maybe one of us should sleep in Jamie's room until then.''

Dakota sat on the edge of the bed, black eyes glittering. Rather than mock him, the floral quilt and lace-trimmed pillows intensified his dark virility. "No. I want to hold you at night. Listen to you breathe and feel your heartbeat.''

She smiled. Such romantic words from the devil-may-care cowboy. "I want that, too."

Dakota removed his boots and let them fall where they may. Annie opened the dresser for her nightgown of choice: an elegant creme silk. As she slipped the garment across her arm and headed toward the bathroom to change, Dakota caught her attention.

"Squirt?"

She turned. "Yes?"

"Don't go. Let me watch you undress this time." His voice was raspy, but nonetheless passionate. "I swear I'll keep my promise. I just want to see you."

Regardless of the weakening of her knees, she fingered the top button on her dress. Refusing his request didn't feel like a viable option. She couldn't turn away from her husband even if she wanted to. She had agreed to be intimate with him. It was too late to act shy now.

"Okay," she said, struggling to raise her voice above the cadence of her heart. "I'll stay."

Nine

Dakota realized Annie had never undressed in front of a captive male before. Her hands quivered as they moved down each button.

"Are you going to just sit there and stare at me?" she asked.

He fought back a grin. Did she expect him to turn away? What would be the point in that? "'Fraid so, squirt."

Her hand stilled. "Please don't ask me to do a striptease."

"Wouldn't dream of it." He'd been to a couple of strip joints and the phony sensuality had done nothing for him. Those women didn't have Annie's elegance or her innocence. He decided not to mention that, though. He didn't frequent topless bars. He'd been to a few bachelor parties and had gotten drunk and watched the show with the rest of the guys. No big deal.

She let the dress slide off her shoulders and pool at her feet. When she reached down to pick it up, Dakota smiled. Her breasts practically spilled out of that skimpy thing she called a bra. Without even trying, she was sexier than any exotic dancer he'd ever seen. Avoiding his gaze, she moved about the room as though trying to pretend he wasn't there.

Dakota's heartbeat quickened. Besides the flimsy black bra, she wore bikini-cut panties and dark stockings attached to a garter belt. Platinum hair, fair skin and bits of silk and lace. What a fantasy. The cowboy boots added a provocative touch, he mused. He loved to see a woman's legs in boots.

As Annie sat on the vanity stool, slipped off her boots and released the suspender hooks on the garter belt, Dakota swallowed. She extended each leg and rolled the hose down in a luxurious motion. She reminded him of one of those movie stars from the forties, a curvaceous figure and silky white hair falling over one eye.

Next, she removed the garter belt and unhooked her bra. She'd turned her back to him, but he could see her reflection in the mirror. He'd already touched her breasts earlier, kissed and tasted them, but he hadn't seen their form or color in a bright light. She was full and lush, crested with pale-pink tips. Dakota licked his lips. Damn if he didn't want another sample.

Down boy, an inner voice warned. *You vowed to keep your promise.* His groin ached like hell, but he liked the idea of the house being vacant the first time they made love. He wanted her relaxed, free of inhibitions. Besides, they both deserved the wedding night they should have had. Romance, candles and flowers. Homemade shampoo and a tub filled with warm, scented water. The whole experience seemed sacred now. Dakota had never made love to a virgin. No woman had ever offered him such a special gift.

Annie stood and slipped the ivory nightgown over her head. Dakota watched it shimmy down her body, wishing his hands could follow. Next she removed her makeup with cleansing cream, cotton pads and a bottle of witch hazel. When that task was complete, she walked over to the dresser and opened the top drawer.

As she retrieved a pair of panties that matched the nightgown, he leaned forward. Much to his disappointment she removed the pair she wore and slid the new ones into place without lifting the hem of her gown.

"That wasn't fair," Dakota complained.

She deposited the discarded panties into a hamper she kept inside the closet. "Don't you start."

"But I wanted to see."

"I did the best I could. This wasn't easy with you watching." Apparently, she had tried to perform her nightly ritual as naturally as she could.

He struggled with his next breath. Wedding night aside, he was hard as a rock and wanting her desperately. Maybe her modesty was a blessing, at least for now.

"I can't help but wonder how blond your curls are," he said in a tone meant to tease, to lighten his own hungry mood. He'd waited years to fulfill his sexual fantasies about her. What was fifteen more days in the scheme of things?

Despite the rosy stain flooding her cheeks, she lifted her chin in a show of defiance. "I don't bleach my hair."

Dakota raised an eyebrow. "Then prove it."

She bent her head and exhibited the part in her hair. "See, no dark roots."

"Smart aleck. You know that's not what I meant."

"Sorry, cowboy." She crossed her arms. "Now it's your turn to get undressed."

He shrugged and pulled open the snaps on his shirt. "I change in front of you all the time."

"But I always look away. Tonight I won't."

Dakota tossed his shirt onto the floor. "How come you haven't looked before?"

She nibbled her bottom lip and lowered her gaze, following the movement of his hand on his belt buckle. "I don't like to tempt myself with things I shouldn't have."

Standing, he flipped open the belt and unzipped his fly. "And now that you've decided to indulge, it's okay to sneak a peek?"

She nodded, and he smiled. She looked as stimulated as he felt. Dakota kicked away his jeans and removed his socks. Without a second thought he peeled off his briefs. "Grab me a pair of boxers, would ya, darlin'?"

She rummaged through his drawer and handed him a blue-striped pair.

"Thanks."

Annie stared appreciatively at his nakedness, taking in every aroused inch. He waited a beat before pulling the boxers on. Their eyes met. "This is how it should be," he said. "Married people should enjoy looking at each other."

She brushed a lock of hair away from her eye. "For a man who never wanted to get married, you sure know a lot about how married people should act."

Although her response caught him off guard, he managed a casual shrug. He didn't know the first thing about how married people should behave. He certainly wasn't the role-model husband. A decent husband would tell his wife about something as important as his upcoming rodeo event.

He rubbed his hand across his jaw, mentally defending his decision to keep silent. If he told her now, the whole issue would probably create a hell of an argument. He knew how stubborn she could be, and he also knew how she felt about his former profession. It would be best to wait, he decided, tell her when the time neared. Maybe by then he'd have an easier time explaining why he needed to ride that bull again. Admitting to a woman that he suffered from anxiety attacks was almost as unmanning as the fear itself.

Annie picked up the shirt he'd left on the floor and tossed it into the hamper. "I know this is a strange time to mention this, but I have a favor to ask of you."

Dakota grabbed his jeans before she could and removed his wallet from the back pocket. "After letting me watch you undress, darlin', you can have anything you want."

"Good." She snagged the jeans along with the rest of his discarded items. "Because I want you to quit smoking."

He nearly choked on his next breath. Anything but that. "Oh, come on, squirt, that's going a little overboard. I've smoked since I was a teenager."

"All the more reason to quit."

"It's my only vice."

"Think about it, Dakota. You go to the gym, swim, ride

horses, do whatever you can to stay healthy and keep in shape. And then you ruin it all by smoking.''

He didn't want to talk logic. "So I enjoy a cigarette now and then. That's not a crime.''

"Now and then?'' She narrowed her eyes. "You smoke at least a pack a day. And besides your health, there are the boys to consider. They idolize you, watch everything you do. How long do you think it will be before one of them decides smoking is cool?''

Why did the woman have to lay a guilt trip on him? "I'll cut back.''

She pressed her index finger into his chest, leaving a temporary imprint. "You'll quit.''

He decided that meeting her halfway would get him off the hook. "I'll try. That's all I can promise.''

"You'll try?'' Annie tilted her head. "This from a man who beat the odds to walk again? I'm disappointed. I thought you were the type who could accomplish anything.''

Damn, she looked cute with her chin in the air and her nipples standing at attention. "You're baiting me, you little minx. Do you think I'm dumb enough to fall for that?''

"How about this? Whenever you crave a cigarette, I'll help you fight the urge by keeping your mouth busy.''

"You'll kiss me?''

She wet her lips. "Tongue and all.''

He moved closer, his pulse throbbing. "Maybe you better take care of me right now. Suddenly, I've got an awful craving.''

A craving that had nothing to do with cigarettes. Fifteen days, he told himself. Just fifteen days. He'd either survive or die trying. A man could certainly freeze to death if he took too many ice-cold showers.

Cursing the gentleman he'd become, he backed away. "Maybe kissing so close to the bed isn't such a good idea. Maybe we ought to play chess or something.''

"Chess?'' Annie sputtered into laughter. The sound was music to his ears. "I hate chess. It's boring.''

"Yeah, I know. But I figure it's better than counting

sheep." *Or fantasizing about all the lusty things I intend to do to you.*

"You're serious?"

"Yep." He searched the top of the closet for the chess board Mary had given him as a joke one Christmas. "Take a seat, darlin'. You're in for the dullest night of your life."

Five days later Dakota leaned against the redwood fence, assessing his surroundings. Horses frolicked in the arena, the wind fluttering through their manes as morning dew tipped each blade of grass. The completed barn had been built just to his specification and Sun Dancer, the palomino gelding he'd found for the kids, behaved like the perfect gentleman.

Dakota scowled. What's wrong with this picture? he asked himself as Mark, the feed-store delivery boy, strode toward him with a cigarette dangling from the corner of his mouth.

Mark handed him a copy of the delivery slip. "You've done a great job with this place."

"Thanks." Dakota stuffed the paper into his pocket and watched the kid light the cigarette. He hadn't taken a hit since Annie had conned him into quitting.

The teenager inhaled, then blew a stream of smoke into the wind. "Hey, did you ever go up to Lookout Point?"

"Yeah, great view. My wife was impressed."

Mark sucked on the cigarette again. "Seems a little weird, a married couple going up there. But then you're like, I don't know, different than most married guys."

Normally Dakota found himself amused by the kid's friendly chatter, but today he envied the sunny-haired, cigarette-toting youth. "How old are you?"

"Eighteen."

The clean-cut kid stood about six feet. An innocent face equipped with a pug nose and twin dimples contradicted his macho stance. Dakota knew the boy admired him some. Mark had been the first person in town to recognize him.

Dakota dug the toe of his boot into the dirt, his voice edged with nicotine-deprived aggravation. "If you're old enough to buy a pack of cigarettes, why are you always bumming them?''

Mark flinched, apparently from the bite in Dakota's tone. He reached into his shirt pocket and held out a crumpled pack. ''I planned on paying you back. You can have the rest if you want.''

Dakota stared at the offering. He'd never wanted anything so badly in his life. Wrong brand, but at this point, he didn't care. ''I'll just take a couple.'' One for now and another for reserve, he thought guiltily. Jamming the filtered-end into his mouth, he cursed his own weakness. ''Sorry I snapped. It's been a rough day.''

Mark tossed him a pack of matches. ''It's cool.''

Dakota's hand nearly shook. *It's not cool at all. I'm a damned addict.* As he pulled the tobacco smoke into his lungs, he decided he would wean himself slowly, one or two smokes a day. Cold turkey didn't appear to be working.

''I guess I'd better go.'' The teenager waved and grinned. ''See ya next time.''

Dakota nodded. ''Yeah, Mark, thanks.''

Leaning against the fence rail, he watched the boy hop into the delivery truck. The cigarette affected him like a drowning man being tossed a life jacket. He inhaled again. Hell, things didn't happen overnight. He couldn't be expected to cure a seventeen-year-old habit in less than a week. Although Annie's kisses tasted sweet, she wasn't always available to curb the craving. He checked his watch. She'd left for work only an hour ago.

Dakota turned toward the arena and admired the geldings. Sun Dancer looked like Roy Rogers's Trigger and moved like a rocking horse, smooth and easy. He'd paid a pretty penny for the palomino, but it was worth it. The kids were turning out to be fine little cowboys, and Sun Dancer suited them well. Dakota smiled. He had the feeling, though, that Jamie would be the rodeo cowboy of the bunch, the saddle bronc rider. Whenever he lifted the two-year-old onto the saddle with him, the child wanted to spur the mount on. ''Faster, Daddy,'' he'd say. ''Make jump.''

One more horse to go, he thought. He already had a mare lined up for Annie.

"Uncle Kody?"

He turned to find Tyler staring up at him, Dog Soldier standing protectively beside the boy. Dakota extinguished the cigarette on the fence rail and dropped it into the dirt, grinding it beneath his heel. From the storm brewing beneath Tyler's glasses, he knew the boy needed to speak his mind. And rightly so. They'd had a family powwow on the danger of smoking, on how it wasn't a cool thing to do.

The child made a fist of both hands. "You promised Annie-Mom you'd quit. You lied to her. And to us."

"I'm sorry. It wasn't a deliberate lie, though. I tried to quit, but I messed up."

"You didn't try very hard."

Dakota took a deep breath. "No, I suppose I didn't. But I'm only human, son. I make mistakes, same as anybody."

Tyler set his jaw. He looked so mature standing there with his hair combed just right and his shirt tucked neatly into his jeans. "My real dad didn't smoke. And he didn't lie, either."

A burning sensation shot through Dakota's eyes. "Your dad was a good man. And I know how much you loved him." Although he had expected a comparison someday, he'd had no idea how badly it would hurt. "I can't be him, Tyler. I can only be me. And I'm sorry if I've disappointed you." *Shattered your confidence by doing something stupid.*

Dakota prayed his eyes wouldn't water and his voice wouldn't crack. Although Tyler knew about the past, about the ceremony that had drawn them together, Dakota felt the need to bare his pitiful soul. "Your real mom was like a sister to me. We made a vow a long time ago to look out for each other. And when she married your dad, he understood that vow and respected it." The child didn't respond, so he continued. "Your dad's acceptance meant a lot. I know I'm nothing like him, but we were friends just the same. He gave me his kids. And you guys are the most important people in the world to me."

Tyler stroked the top of Dog Soldier's head, his expression

wavering between sorrow and confusion. "What about Annie-Mom? Isn't she important to you?"

Dakota stepped forward. "Of course, she is. She's my wife." *My friend, my soon-to-be lover. My obsession.* "We're family. All of us."

"Will you tell her the truth? About your smoking?"

"Yeah." He nodded. "And I shouldn't have asked you guys to keep Maria a secret from your mom. Even though everything worked out okay and your mom wasn't mad, I had no right to do that." And he had no right to keep his future plans from Annie, either. She deserved to know about Excalibur, yet he wasn't prepared to tell her. He needed more time to strengthen their bond, prepare himself to open up to her, admit his fears. "I promise I'll quit smoking. I won't mess up again."

"Okay." The boy shuffled his feet. "Maria's making waffles for breakfast. Do you want some?"

"Sure." The elderly housekeeper had become invaluable. She cooked, cleaned and gave Spanish lessons. Kids and dogs adored her. "I'll be right along."

Tyler turned in the direction of the house, then back again. "I love you, Uncle Kody," he said in a small, forgiving voice.

This time Dakota's eyes filled with tears. He blinked them back and smiled. "I love you, too, son."

Immediately the boy took off running as though the exchange had embarrassed him a little.

Tossing the "reserve" cigarette onto the ground, Dakota watched him go, his own undeserving heart clenching. *I have a lot to learn about being a father,* he thought as Dog Soldier, proud and strong, followed the child with a playful bark.

Annie flinched. "Why do you have to blindfold me?"

Dakota folded the bandanna and brought it toward her eyes. "Because I want you to be surprised."

The sunlight spilling across their bed disappeared as he tied the blindfold into place. His last surprise consisted of three rambunctious dogs. Lord knew what he had in store this time.

He had taken the kids to a neighbor's house so she and Dakota could spend the morning alone.

"Where are we going?" she asked as he took her arm.

"You'll see."

"I can't see anything. I feel as though I'm going to break my neck."

He guided her down what she assumed was the hallway. When their booted feet made noise, she realized they had entered the tiled floor in the kitchen. "Did you make me breakfast? I don't smell any food."

"No. We'll eat later."

She stumbled along, not quite picking up her feet. "Did you buy a new refrigerator or stove or something?"

He laughed. "No, nothing that mundane. Be careful here."

She took a cautious step. When a cool breeze brushed her cheeks, she knew he had led her through the back door and onto the patio. "We're outside."

"Smart girl."

"Don't make fun of me. This is really strange."

He brought her hand to his lips and kissed it. "Relax and enjoy the elements. I'm right here."

Immediately her senses heightened. Dakota's lips felt moist and tender, the beard stubble on his chin slightly abrasive. As they continued, Mother Earth drifted to her nostrils with a heady mix of freshly mowed grass and blooming flowers. The squeak of a hinge told her he had opened the gate that led to the back of the property.

Twigs snapped beneath her feet as she pictured the yard. Rows of trees grew along the borders of the acreage, offering greenery and shade. In the forefront, a circular pipe corral served as the primary training area for the children's riding lessons, while Dakota's roping arena and cattle pens dominated the left side of the property. In the rear, a barn, equipped with six box stalls, a well-stocked tack room and a feed-storage area provided Western charm. Behind the barn, a dirt path led to the horse trail shared by the ranch community.

As a gentle wind teased Annie's hair, she imagined Dakota's locks lifting in disarray.

"Are we almost there?" she asked, noticing the ground felt harder beneath her feet.

Boyish excitement sounded in his voice. "Just arrived."

Annie inhaled. "I smell hay and horses."

Dakota held her still. "We're in the barn."

"Is my surprise in here?"

"Yes."

Dakota's lips brushed hers as his arms circled her waist. Although she normally closed her eyes while kissing, being blindfolded evoked a wicked sensation. Relying on her sense of touch, she lifted her hands and explored. His hair felt as tousled as she had imagined, thick and glorious.

Their tongues merged as a horse whinnied. Dakota pushed Annie against a solid surface and deepened the kiss. As his hands roamed, she gasped. He toyed aggressively with the buttons on her blouse, his fingertips brushing her nipples.

"Are you going to undress me?" The possibility that his surprise might be a sexual ravishing thrilled yet frightened her. He had her at a vulnerable disadvantage. Their "honeymoon" wasn't until next weekend.

He nipped her bottom lip. "Truthfully, I hadn't planned on it, but if you want me to, I'd be happy to oblige."

"You didn't bring me out here to make love?"

She heard his breath catch. "You have a delicious imagination. I'll keep that in mind the next time I blindfold you." He skimmed her cheek with a callused finger. "But I think we should make our first encounter a little more conventional. You know, save the kinky stuff for later." He brought his finger to her lips and traced their shape. "Then again, maybe not. Forget predictability. We're gonna go on roller-coaster ride next weekend, darlin'. Make love whenever and wherever the mood strikes. Live out our fantasies."

Annie knew she must be blushing. Apparently she did have an overactive imagination, one that had triggered his. She reached for the bandanna, hoping he was teasing her. She didn't want to lose her virginity on a fast, lusty ride. Predictability suited her just fine. "Can I take this off now?"

A smile sounded in his voice. "Sure."

She released the blindfold and stared straight ahead. In the stall directly in front of her stood one of the most beautiful horses she had ever seen. All it needed was a set of big, fluffy wings to classify it as a mythical creature. The animal was as white as snow, with a luxurious mane. Although Annie wasn't an equine expert, she thought it probably had a near-perfect confirmation. An attractive-shaped head sat upon a sleek, well-crested neck.

"This has to be a mare," she said. The horse appeared to carry itself with well-deserved feminine pride, too pretty for a gelding, too serene for a stallion.

Dakota grinned and stepped forward. "Her name's Marilyn. And I think she enjoyed watching us kiss."

Annie patted the mare's neck, delighting in the nuzzling response. "Marilyn? As in Monroe?"

"Yeah, that's actually her registered name. "Marilyn 'Norma Jean' Monroe. It fits, don't you think?"

"It's perfect." The mare probably drove the stallions crazy, just the way her namesake had affected a generation of human males. "She's gorgeous."

"I had a feeling you'd think so. She's a great horse. Gentle, loyal, professionally trained. She has that rare quality to adjust to the rider's needs. She could take a beginner a long way."

"Did you buy her?"

"Not yet. But I will if you want me to. Of course, I'd expect you to ride her before you decide." He appraised Marilyn with a smile. "She belongs to a trainer in town. I had mentioned that I was looking for a horse for my wife, and one connection led to another."

Annie leaned over the stall opening and studied the mare again. Marilyn looked as though she belonged in a parade or in a show ring. "I can't accept a horse like this. She should go to someone who knows what they're doing. She's too glamorous for trail riding."

Dakota shook his head. "Don't sell yourself short. You might be inexperienced, but you're a good rider." He reached for Annie's hair and brought a thick strand to his lips. "And you're a beautiful woman. You deserve a beautiful horse."

"Thank you." The man certainly knew how to charm a lady. A God-given gift, she thought. He didn't even have to try. "But don't you think it would be wasting Marilyn's flash to use her as a trail horse?"

"No." Dakota released Annie's hair and watched it flutter across her shoulders. "Just because something is beautiful doesn't mean it has to be put on display. Look at you. You don't flaunt your flash."

She knew he considered her platinum hair and abundant curves her "flash." Being thought of as a bombshell didn't suit her personality or her life-style, yet Dakota had presented her with an exquisite horse, aptly named after a sex symbol.

Now wasn't the time to go into that, though. Not with Marilyn gazing at Annie through adoring blue eyes. The mare appeared to be waiting to see if she had found a new home. Annie's heart warmed. How could she refuse such a special gift?

"I'd like to ride her."

"Great." Dakota spun on his heel, grinning. "She's already been lunged. Lead her outside and I'll get the tack."

Annie entered the stall and slipped a halter onto Marilyn. "Be patient with me," she whispered to the mare. "I'm not sure if I even remember how to saddle a horse correctly. It's been a few years."

As it turned out, she remembered just fine. Mounting the horse, she thought about her dad and his broken promise—the pony she had longed for as a child. Strange how Dakota always seemed to be making up for her father's mistakes.

He sat on the arena fence and watched as she took Marilyn through her gaits. With the wind fluttering through her hair and bits of alfalfa dusting the air, Annie appreciated the mare's cooperation. The responsive horse brought on an eagerness to improve her riding skills.

As Annie neared her husband, she checked the mare's reins. The horse stopped immediately. "Will you work with me, Dakota? Teach me to be a better rider?"

His face lit up. Today he wore various shades of denim and time-worn boots. "Does that mean you want Marilyn?"

Annie nodded. "Yes. She's terrific."

The mare had to be expensive, but she wouldn't dare ask Dakota about the price. They kept separate bank accounts. Aside from the trust funds he'd started for the kids, she wasn't privy to his finances. She didn't think he kept his accounts private out of selfishness, though. Not only did Dakota insist on paying the monthly bills, he was more than charitable with personal gifts and improvements on the house.

Dakota's voice brought her back to the topic at hand: horse-back riding. "I'd be glad to work with you, squirt, but truthfully, I think it would make more sense to hire a trainer for both you and the kids."

She cocked her head. "Why?"

"A couple of reasons." He scraped the toe of his boot against the fence rail. "First of all, just because I can ride doesn't mean I can teach. I've been doing all right with the boys, but I think they'd improve faster with a professional trainer. And so would you."

Dakota rearranged his already-tousled hair in his typical fashion and continued the explanation. "And second, I may not be around all that much. Of course, I promise not to leave you in a lurch. I'll hire a ranch hand to help out."

Disappointment spoiled the magic of his gift. Unfortunately she had been feeling possessive of Dakota these days. And even though she knew their upcoming lovemaking was the cause, she couldn't help it. She didn't like envisioning him on the road, away from her and the children. "Do you plan on traveling that much?"

"Yeah. I've got something in the works that may take a lot of my time."

Why did he always have to be so vague? "What?"

He shrugged. "I'm just kicking around some ideas for a new business venture. There's no point in going into it right now."

Whatever it was, he'd made sure it involved being on the road, she thought grimly. "The boys will miss you." She knew it was a cheap shot to try to keep him home, but at the moment she didn't care.

"They'll adjust. Children adapt easily, or so I've heard."

Apparently wives didn't, though. She was already too used to having him around. "When you're ready to work out the details on your business plan, let me know. I'd be glad to help."

"Thanks." He hopped off the fence. "You know, I had planned on going to a powwow next month by myself, but I think maybe you and the boys should come along. I'm sure we'll be due for a family outing by then."

Annie smiled and combed her fingers through the horse's mane. Some of the magic, it seemed, had just returned. A family outing was just what they needed.

Ten

     ─────

The following Saturday Annie pulled into the garage, turned off the ignition and massaged her temples. She had just returned from chaos—dropping the kids off at Mary's house for the weekend. Jamie had insisted on bringing Jeremiah the bulldog along, which of course meant Taco the Chihuahua had to go, too. Only Dog Soldier seemed satisfied to stay behind, but the mixed-breed dog didn't sleep in a bed and eat table scraps, either. Dog Soldier accepted the fact that he was a dog.

She exited the gold minivan, then leaned against it, taking in her surroundings. The three-car garage had certainly undergone a transformation. Drywall, a fresh coat of paint, several windows and a workshop had been added. It was actually pleasant, in a masculine sort of way. Dakota might not keep the house in order, but his workshop sported organized shelves, white cabinetry and a well-stocked, professionally built jeweler's bench.

She looked up as the door from the house opened and Dakota strolled through it.

"Hi, darlin'." He flashed a crooked grin. "How'd it go?"

Annie crossed her arms. She'd just spent forty-five minutes in bumper-to-bumper traffic with three kids and two puppies, and he wanted to know how it went. He could have offered to make the trip instead of doing God-knew-what. "Miles and Tyler argued over the radio station the entire time. Clearly a waste of effort since they couldn't hear the music, anyway, not through Jeremiah's snores and Taco's high-pitched yips."

She dropped her purse onto the ground and studied Dakota.

As he jammed the corner of a red cloth deeper into his front pocket, it waved against his thigh, drawing her attention to his jeans. Holes and frayed seams decorated the faded denim. He looked gorgeous in a rugged, guy-in-the-garage kind of way. Black boots and equally black hair offered sexy rebellion while a bare chest and washboard stomach rippled with muscle.

"So what have you been doing?" she asked.

"Detailing my truck. Want to see?"

It was their honeymoon weekend, and he was detailing his truck? "Not really."

"Come on, squirt. It will only take a second."

Annie picked up her purse and followed him to the other side of the garage. An open toolbox and jars of cleaning supplies sat beneath the gleaming Ford. Several rags, much like the one in his pocket, were scattered about.

"It looks good," she said, wondering what she was supposed to notice. He always kept it spotless.

"Do you wanna climb into the bed and neck?"

She rolled her eyes. "Dakota."

"I'm serious. You look gorgeous. Wild and windblown. Perfect for the back of a truck."

Annie wouldn't have described her disheveled appearance as gorgeous. Besides a messy ponytail, she wore a slightly wrinkled summer-cotton dress and leather sandals. She twisted a strand of hair self-consciously. Did he honestly want to make love in the back of his truck? "Are you teasing me?"

Dakota released the barrette that held her ponytail. The metal ornament clanked as it hit the cement floor. Ruffling the blond mass, he watched it tumble over her shoulders. "What do you think?"

As he reached for the top button of the dress, her heartbeat accelerated. The floral-printed garment sported tiny pearl buttons. Dakota's fingers appeared exceptionally large next to them. One by one he freed each opaque pearl, his movements slow and calculated.

After the dress slipped from her shoulders, their eyes met. Annie breathed deeply, exhaling on a ragged sigh. Regardless of predictability, she had envisioned making love in a dimly lit bedroom, their bodies nestled between silk and lace. And she'd planned on being stripped of an elegant nightgown, but from the fevered look on Dakota's face, none of that mattered.

He stepped back to view her, his eyes taking in every feminine curve. Predator's eyes, she thought. Dark and ravenous. As he lowered his chin, he rolled his shoulders. Muscles bunched and coiled.

"You're so beautiful," he said, his gaze following the arch of her neck, the fullness of her breasts. "So damn beautiful."

With her dress pooling at her feet and her hair lovingly mussed, she stood before her husband in a blush-pink bra and panty set, her nipples straining, her legs slightly parted. He made her feel beautiful. Beautiful and a little afraid.

In one sleek motion the predator pounced, closing the gap between them. Banding her arms, he pressed her against the truck. The flash of chrome grazed her skin.

Catching her hips between his hands, he rubbed the bulge beneath his fly against the front of her panties. The friction from the denim felt rough and oddly sensual, as untamed as the man. Electricity shot from his sex to hers, like lightning in a storm. Trapped in the downpour, she rocked her hips and gripped his bare shoulders, her fingertips imprinting on his skin. In turn, he seared her exposed flesh with hot, openmouthed kisses.

Annie reveled in the madness, the hunger and the want. The scent of arousal misted their bodies like rain from a waterfall, but when she reached down to unzip his jeans, he pulled away.

He expelled a heavy breath, then tugged his hands through

his hair. "If you touch me, it will end too soon. It's been a long time. Too damn long."

Annie caught her bottom lip between her teeth. "But isn't this what you want?" A fast, lusty ride? Why else would he have undressed her in the garage?

Dakota flashed his signature smile—the one decidedly lopsided and unconsciously alluring. "Sure, but this is your honeymoon, too. And I think you should pick the fantasy."

She traced the crooked tilt of his lips. They were still moist. "I want whatever you want."

He kissed the tip of her finger. "Not true. You want what every first-time bride wants. Romance, flowers, candles."

She couldn't deny his claim, because deep down she had always longed for a conventional wedding night. "But you said that was predictable."

"I did?" He lifted her into his arms and carried her through the open doorway and into the house. "Well, what can I say, darlin'?" The lopsided grin returned. "Except I lied."

As Dakota carried Annie into their bedroom, beauty surrounded her. Vanilla-scented candles, dozens of them, flickered among tall vases of white roses. The bed had been made up with silk sheets, and a heart-shaped pillow trimmed in lace rested in the center, a single red rose placed upon it as a romantic offering.

The whitewashed dresser displayed a crystal ice bucket, a bottle of sparkling cider and a frothy cake decorated with sugared roses and a row of succulent strawberries.

Annie gazed up at her husband as he placed her on the edge of the bed. Tears gathered in her eyes. "You are the most incredible man. Do you know how much this means to me?"

He shrugged somewhat shyly, and she smiled. The torn jeans and scuffed boots made him look like a renegade who had kidnapped someone else's bride, but the flickering candlelight enhanced the handsome angles of his face. He, like everything else, was perfect.

Annie fingered the sheets. "You weren't really detailing

your truck, were you? It was a setup so I wouldn't catch on to your surprise."

"Yeah, I planned it." He smiled again. "But the part where I undressed you, that just kind of happened. And I've got the feeling it's going to happen a lot. I don't think I'll be able to keep my hands to myself from now on."

And such capable hands they were, she thought. Strong, masculine and clean. His jeans were old and worn, but his skin looked freshly showered, not at all like a man who'd been working in the garage. "I thought your truck seemed the same."

"Oh, yeah. Now you say that. Now that you know the truth." Dakota kicked off his boots and opened the cider. "I was going to get champagne, but I wanted us to be in control of our senses. Tonight is a gift. A blessing. In my culture, a woman losing her virginity is sacred."

She smiled and reached out to him. He couldn't have said anything that would have pleased her more. How perfect could one man be?

Too perfect, her subconscious answered. Too right. Too handsome. Too alluring. "I think I'm falling into your trap."

"This isn't a trap, Annie. I'm your husband."

"I know, I'm sorry. I didn't mean—"

He kissed her apology away, stealing her skepticism with it. When they came up for air, their eyes met.

"Can we feed each other?" she asked. "The way brides and grooms are supposed to?"

"We can do anything you want." He lowered his voice to a husky whisper. "Absolutely anything."

Immediately Annie's nipples tightened. She sliced a piece of cake and slid it onto a plate. Scanning the dresser, she noticed the absence of eating utensils. "There aren't any forks."

"Really? Guess I must have forgot."

Annie dipped her finger into the frosting, catching a portion of a fluffy red rose. From the mischievous look on his face, she assumed he had forgotten purposely.

Deliberately playful, they took turns feeding each other. She nibbled his fingers, he licked icing from her lips. She watched him swallow, he traced her cleavage with a line of cider.

Annie arched her neck, and he followed the liquid path with his tongue.

She reveled in his touch, his texture, their differences. His hair sparkled like midnight, hers glittered with sunshine. He was hard where she was soft, dark where she was fair. His beard stubble scraped the curve of her breasts. Her fingernails massaged his scalp.

Dakota reached behind her and unhooked her bra. The garment went slack. He removed it, raised his head and smiled. As he dipped his finger into the cider, she sat perfectly still, her heart thundering.

"Dakota, you're not going to—"

But he did.

Circling her nipples, he moistened each one, covering them with pearls of the sparkling liquid. Annie trembled with exquisite anticipation. He reminded her of a jungle cat with his long body and rangy muscles—a powerful creature who had just discovered his mate.

As Dakota lowered his mouth and caught the clinging beads with his tongue, Annie mewled like his female counterpart.

They were surrounded by fire, she realized, dancing circles of red and gold. The room blazed with beauty—beauty he had created.

Dakota placed his head against her heart. She felt the beats intensify.

"Lie down, Annie. Let me love you."

She reached for the rose he had left her and sank her head into a pillow. He leaned forward and fanned out her hair.

"Even when you were a little girl, I wanted to touch your hair, see if it was as soft as it looked."

She lifted the flower and stroked his cheek with the petals. "I would have died on the spot."

"I know. You had a terrible crush on me." He brushed his mouth across hers. "But I was too old for you."

Annie touched her tongue to his lips. He tasted as perfect

as he looked—sparkling cider, sugared roses and man. "And you were much too wild."

As he gazed down at her, his eyes shimmered like black diamonds and his hair fell across his forehead in natural disarray. He was still too wild, she thought. A sleek, powerful panther fighting the cage that confined him.

She knew he would never be hers, not completely. But she hoped and prayed that he wouldn't disappoint her someday. Let her down the way all the other men in her life had. Promises led to dreams; broken vows led to heartache.

"We don't really belong to each other," she said, her thoughts drifting into words.

He ran his hands down the sides of her body, following the curve of her waist, flare of her hips. "Tonight we will." Reversing his caress, he skimmed her breasts, igniting each nipple. "In most Indian cultures, a man and woman aren't really married until they make love."

Annie reached for Dakota's hands and placed them against the waistband of her panties, inviting him to remove the last of her clothing. God help her, but tonight she wanted to be married. Married to him.

He slid the pink satin from her hips and knelt between her thighs. "Lift your legs onto my shoulders," he whispered. "Let me have my fantasy."

Although a sudden wave of shyness washed over her, she didn't protest. Annie scooted forward and lowered her lashes. "No one has ever— I've never let anyone…"

"Good." He stroked the inside of her thighs. "I've been waiting so long for this. For us."

As he lowered his mouth and kissed her, she shivered and opened her eyes to watch, brushing an errant lock from his forehead. A golden warmth flooded through her. Beautiful, wild Dakota, she thought.

As he deepened the kiss, she gasped, filling her lungs with sweetly scented smoke, sex and man. She had become one with the fire, the flames illuminating the room.

The exploration of his tongue swept through her, heating

the passion. She touched his face, his lips and even his tongue as it teased her core and delved deeper.

Blood roared in her ears and pulsed through her veins. Streams of light burned her eyes and misted her vision. She was drugged by his power, trapped by her own sensuality. She wanted it to last forever, yet she wanted it to end.

Annie writhed beneath him, clutching handfuls of his hair, begging him to stop, pleading for him to continue. He glanced up at her, and she shuddered and arched. His mouth was damp and warm, desperate to please.

On the brink of madness she trapped his gaze and moved against him, gasping his name through ragged breaths. Relentless, he urged her on until she sobbed and splintered into a thousand glorious pieces.

Annie rode the crest with exquisite pleasure. The room swirled around her, the familiar sights blurred by a kaleidoscope of color.

As Dakota settled in beside her, she dropped her head onto a pillow and struggled to focus. When she grabbed hold of the sheet, the silk slipped through her fingers like water.

He moved closer, his long, muscular body cool and slick. At what point he had removed his jeans, she wasn't sure. But what she could attest to was the fact that he was naked and fully aroused.

She turned her head and brushed his cheek with a tender kiss. He nuzzled her neck, then rose above her, his eyes glazed with passion.

Dakota smiled at the woman beneath him, the woman he had craved for so long. She looked sweet yet sexy—a fluffy little kitten high on catnip and cream. She had no idea how beautiful she was, he thought. How innocently sensual. A part of him wanted to take her hard and fast, but the other part, the husband in him, wanted to savor her forever.

He skimmed his fingers over her breasts and through the blond waves tangled around them. Needing more, he pulled a strand of her hair into his mouth and feasted on her nipples.

She made a sound, a mewling noise, and drew him closer.

His erection brushed her thigh, and she shivered. "Can I touch you?" she asked, trailing a hand down his stomach.

He felt his muscles jump. How many years had he dreamed of this? Envisioned every sensual detail? "Please, yes."

She explored him innocently, passionately. A woman's claim—gentle yet possessive.

He moved against her hand, encouraging her to tighten her grip. "I want you so badly."

She rubbed her thumb over him, over a drop of moisture seeping from the tip. "I want you, too."

Annie parted her thighs and Dakota settled between them. Covering her hand with his, he guided himself to her.

Warm, wet heat surrounded him.

He caught his breath and groaned.

She buried her face against his shoulder in what seemed like a cross between discomfort and joy, a woman accepting a man for the first time. But as Dakota thrust deeper, she tensed, then gasped in pain.

Immediately he stilled. Even though the nature of her pain was to be expected, her wounded cry shot through him like an arrow.

"This is a first for me, too," he whispered, offering the only comfort he had to give. "I've never touched a woman flesh to flesh." He'd always used protection in the past, guarded himself with a veil of latex. Tonight, though, he couldn't. He needed to feel her, just this once.

Annie's features softened. "Flesh to flesh," she said, shifting her hips as though searching for pleasure beneath the pain.

Dakota waited and watched, allowing her time to explore their joining, the sensation of tangled limbs, the unfamiliar weight of an aroused man.

But when she moved again, stirring him, he closed his eyes and struggled to control the urge to plunge hard and deep, satisfy his own selfish need.

They remained silent for a time, he with his eyes closed, she experimenting beneath him. One more rock of her hips, he thought, and he was going to swoop down on her like a vicious animal.

"Dakota?"

He opened his eyes. "What, darlin'?"

"You feel incredible."

He grinned—a proud, overwhelmed grin. "Yeah?"

"Yeah."

Lifting her hips, she accepted every swollen inch, sheathing him like a tight glove. Together they found a sinuous rhythm, a rippling, sensual current.

Filled with the need to give pleasure, he fought the masculine urge to take. Annie's passion had bewitched him. Candlelight played over her skin and glowed in her eyes. As he increased the tempo, the pressure building in his loins threatened to erupt.

She was wild and erotic. The lover he knew she would be. The woman he'd fantasized about. The wife he couldn't seem to get enough of. She writhed and purred, thrashed and clawed—as needy and untamed as he.

Teetering on control, he swallowed. "Do you know what you're doing to me?"

She wet her lips, pressed her mouth to his ear and began to shudder against him. "The same thing you're..."

Her breathy climax was his undoing. A red haze fogged his mind and glazed his eyes. Fire. Flames of desire. An inferno of urgency. Dakota thrust harder, deeper, faster, until every fantasy he'd ever had about Annie crashed over him like a violent tidal wave. With a guttural cry, he flung back his head and poured everything he was, everything he had, into the woman beneath him.

Several silent moments later Dakota studied Annie's tender expression, stunned by the power of his release. Making love with her had been everything he had imagined. Everything and more.

She stroked his back. "Lie down. Let me hold you."

"No, darlin'. I want to hold you." He shifted their positions, and she relaxed almost bonelessly against him. He wrapped his arms around her. Should he tell her how important she had become to him? That their lovemaking felt like more than just sex? He actually enjoyed being married. Maybe enjoyed it too much. He had this awful feeling that he'd miss Annie when he went on the road.

Dakota frowned. Why was she so important? So vital to his life?

Because, he told himself hastily, he had spent too many years running wild, and now Annie was his salvation, his chance to prove himself, redeem the man he used to be.

He closed his eyes. There was, of course, one part of his past Annie couldn't fix. She couldn't erase the image he had of himself broken and bleeding. Motionless and afraid. She couldn't take his anxiety away—the fears that had come with his accident.

I have to go back, he told himself, defending his decision to ride Excalibur. *I have to.*

"What's wrong?" she asked. "You're so quiet."

Quiet and tense, he realized. His secrets were weighing on him. Secrets, half-truths, omissions he wasn't ready to reveal.

"Nothing, I'm fine." He wrapped his arms tighter around her, pulling himself back into the moment, the luxury of being with her. "I made some herbal soap," he said, resuming his role as her husband once again. "Shampoo, too."

She reached for his hand. "You did?"

He nodded. It was his duty to cleanse her body after love-making, wash away the maiden's blood. Virginity was revered in his culture. Cheyenne women used to wear protective ropes as chastity belts, a highly respected practice. Dakota couldn't help but cherish the gift Annie had given him.

"Do you want to soak in the tub?" he asked. "We can burn some sage, maybe bathe by candlelight."

"Mmm." She moaned dreamily against him. "That sounds heavenly."

The oversize claw-footed bathtub brimmed with warm water and fragrant oils. Annie closed her eyes as Dakota shampooed her hair. She sat in front of him, between his drawn-up knees. His deft fingers massaged her scalp, working the suds into a rich lather. He had already washed her body, soothing the soreness their lovemaking had caused.

His chivalry surprised her. She had never expected a man like Dakota to honor a woman's choice to protect her virginity for so long. He was far more conventional than she could have ever imagined. Romantic and generous, too. A traditional Cheyenne.

"Why did you buy Marilyn for me?" she asked, suddenly wondering about the significance of the horse and the connection to Dakota's culture.

He continued to massage her scalp, but his response sounded almost shy. "I know you've always enjoyed riding. Besides, in the old days it was customary for a warrior to send horses to a young woman's lodge. It was part of the marriage proposal."

Annie smiled. Just as she suspected, he had been courting her, preparing her for their wedding night. He had even made two shampoos, an inky-black one for his hair and a pale-gold for hers.

How could this reckless cowboy have turned into such a caring husband and a protective father? Annie closed her eyes. And just how long would the splendor last? She was familiar with Dakota's culture. As traditional as they were, Cheyenne marriages were not set in stone. Divorce was permitted.

Mary had accused her of being in love, but Annie knew that wasn't so. Most women became attached to their first lovers. It was natural, this feeling she had for him. This strange ache. He had been a part of her life for eighteen years, and now he had become her husband, the man she'd given her virginity to. She had the right to melt a little.

Dakota piled her damp hair on top of her head and kissed the back of her neck. A shiver slid from her spine to the tip of her toes. She recalled how his mouth looked against her skin, how hungry and wild.

As he tongued her ear, her nipples tightened. "I like having my hair washed."

"And I like touching you," he answered, turning to brush her lips with his.

Melting, she decided, didn't begin to describe the sensation he evoked. She wanted to touch him, too. All over.

"When do I get to wash your hair?" she asked, anxious to run her hands through the thick, glossy strands. The ends brushing his nape already glistened with beads of water.

"After I rinse yours."

She scooted toward the brass spigot, and he grabbed hold of the shower-massage attachment. Running warm water through it, he sprayed a heavy stream over her hair. Suds liquefied and flowed down her shoulders, scenting her skin with chamomile, marigold and orange flowers.

After the invigorating rinse, Dakota applied a clear conditioner to her hair, then kissed her. But this time when he lifted the shower massage, water rained over both of them, sprinkling their faces while they kissed.

Soon they switched places and Dakota settled between her parted legs, the broad expanse of his back before her. Annie adjusted her legs, elevating herself to a kneeling position, instead. Dakota's head was too high to reach otherwise.

Although his hair was heavy and straight, the multisheared layers created sexy disarray, even when damp. His homemade shampoo was thick and dark, a scented indigo blend. Annie applied a dollop and treated him to the same gentle massage which he had bestowed upon her.

The antique tub accommodated them well, and she decided that from this moment on, sharing baths would become part of their nightly ritual.

As Annie reached for the shower attachment, Dakota stopped her. "I think we'd better drain the tub so I can rinse under the regular shower. The dye in my shampoo is pretty strong. It might stain the porcelain if it doesn't get washed down right away."

"Okay." She pulled the plug and stood back while he adjusted the shower nozzle.

After most of the water had drained, Dakota ducked under the shower head and proceeded to rinse his hair.

Annie watched through appreciative eyes. The shampoo trailed from the ends of his hair and onto his shoulders in a dark watery line. As he raised his arms, rock-hard biceps bulged.

God, he was built. Angular bones. Raw sinew. Muscle. She noticed Dakota had been spending more time on all of his physical activities. He had lengthened his gym routine and increased the hours he normally spent on horseback. Lately his rigorous workout could be compared to that of an athlete in training. Annie decided his compulsion to keep in shape stemmed from habit, rather than necessity. After all, a paralyzing accident had forced him into early retirement. He was no longer a professional athlete.

Dakota continued to rinse the shampoo until the water dripping from his hair streamed down his chest in clear, colorless lines.

Annie stepped forward and joined him under the shower. "Can I touch you?" she asked, pressing her lips against his ear in order to be heard above the pounding water.

He softened the spray by adjusting the nozzle; it misted gently, almost seductively. "You don't have to keep asking for permission to put your hands on me."

She sent him a mischievous grin. "My hands? Who said anything about my hands?" Dakota's eyes widened, and she nibbled her smile. "Don't you remember our date, the night we necked in the truck?" The night she had gotten him hot and bothered by admitting what she wanted to do to him. Her mouth and his anatomy. She remembered shocking him senseless. "As I recall, you rather liked the idea."

"Liked it?" He pulled her tight against him. "It was one of the most erotic moments of my life. I've thought about it every day since, picturing what you were going to do to me. Wondering how it would feel."

Empowered by his admission, she slid to her knees. He cupped her face and lowered his head to watch.

"Annie," he whispered, his voice husky and aroused. "My sweet Annie."

As she took him into her mouth, he groaned and guided her, intensifying the heat, the masculine taste. The feminine thrill. He grew hard and thick, fully aroused and pulsing with life.

She licked and teased and stroked, then worked her way back up his body, kissing as she went.

When she reached his lips, he kissed her back, hard and deep, hungry but controlled. He slipped his hand between her thighs, then gentled the pressure of his mouth. "Are you still sore?" he asked.

Annie shook her head, touched by his concern, his ability to contain the primal urges she saw brewing in his eyes.

"I'm fine," she answered, nuzzling his neck, tasting the moisture beading on his skin, the steam that rose all around them. She wanted him as much as he wanted her.

Predictability no longer applied. Not when it referred to this man. This incredible, perfect man. Her husband. Her first-time lover. She wanted him in ways she couldn't begin to count.

She wrapped her legs around him while he entered her, his breath ragged, his body hard and slick. Together they kissed and panted and made wondrous love.

A joining that propelled them past a million glittering stars and beyond.

A joining Annie never wanted to end.

Eleven

Annie had attended powwows before, but being with her family made this traditional gathering even more special. As they relaxed on the lawn with the rest of the spectators, the summer sun sparkled through the trees. The public park reigned over acres of farmland. In the valley below, grazing cattle looked like dark patches in an enchanted world of green.

Moments before The Grand Entry began, the crowd was asked to stand. Dakota removed his Stetson and Jamie gazed up at him.

"Why you do that?" the two-year-old asked.

Dakota picked up his son. "The flag bearers are coming into the arena. See?"

A tall man with long braids carried The Eagle Staff as an elderly man in brilliant regalia supported the American flag. Miles and Tyler placed their hands upon their hearts as red, white and blue waved in the breeze.

Jamie, clinging comfortably to Dakota, appeared awed by his surroundings. Just as a procession of male dancers entered the grassy arena, the little boy gasped. Annie understood why.

Head gear ranged from animal pelts to full-feather head-dresses. Breastplates, constructed of bone and sinew, spanned masculine chests while angora-fur anklets, adorned with shiny silver bells, chimed merrily. Whereas some participants wore breech cloths and body paint, others proudly displayed ribbon shirts and feather bustles, one at their waists, the other suspended between their shoulder blades.

As a striking young man paraded by with a roach of porcupine quills attached to his headband, Jamie leaned over and pointed to the top of his brother's spiked hair. "Him look like Miles."

Dakota and Annie exchanged a parental grin, then watched the procession, which by this time included colorfully clad women and children. As the participants wound around the arena in a clockwise motion, the boys bombarded Dakota with questions.

"Why are they wearing numbers?" Miles asked.

Dakota explained that the dancers competed for prize money, and that their regalia, sometimes handed down through generations, represented their Nation and style of dance.

"That's a Traditional Dancer," he said, motioning to a man in a breech cloth and moccasins who carried a war shield. "He depicts a warrior preparing for battle. That's why his face and body are painted." Shifting Jamie in his arms, he pointed to a teenage girl in an ornately beaded taffeta dress and long-fringed shawl. "She'll be competing in The Fancy Shawl Dance. See how she spins around with her shawl?"

"Me want to dance," Jamie said, seeming mesmerized by the twirling girl.

Dakota nuzzled the two-year-old's cheek. "We'll all get to, later."

Tyler looked up at his dad with a worried expression. "How can we? We don't know the steps, and we're not wearing the right clothes."

Dakota touched the boy's shoulder. "We won't be competing, just dancing for fun. And you don't have to know the steps. There's no right or wrong in the Friendship Dance."

Tyler adjusted his glasses and smoothed his slicked hair,

gestures that made him appear far older than his eight years. Annie had always considered him an old soul, wisdom in a child's body. Today, though, shyness masked all that wisdom.

Tyler gazed out at the arena. "I'm not sure I want to go out there."

Dakota responded softly. "You can decide when the time comes. The choice is yours."

Miles, different from his older brother in almost every way, volunteered eagerly. "I'll go. It looks fun."

At that moment Annie realized the boys didn't remember details about the powwows they'd attended with their parents. Jill had taken them to several, but apparently too many years had passed.

"It is fun," she said. "And both of you danced when you were little. Your mom used to take you out there. And she convinced me to try it, too."

Tyler cocked his head. Annie knew he liked to be reminded about his relationship with his biological parents. He prayed for them every night, asked God to take care of them. His voice gained a pitch of confidence. "Maybe I'll do it. You know, since everyone else is."

The Flag Song and blessing invocation silenced Annie's encouraging response. She stood quietly out of respect. After The Eagle Staff and flags were set to rest near the announcer's booth, the spectators resumed their seats.

Tyler scooted closer to Annie, while Miles and Jamie shared Dakota's lap. They spent the next hour companionably watching the dancers, but when Jamie began to fidget, Dakota glanced over at his wife. "I think it's time to check out the craft booths. Our youngest is ready for a change of scenery."

While strolling along with Jamie attached to her hip, Annie studied her husband. With his sleeves rolled up and his hat dipped low, he moved at a relaxed pace, a cowboy on Indian time, his steel-gray boots skimming dirt patches in the grass. Stopping often to chat with jewelers and traders about their merchandise, he collected business cards. He also smiled charmingly, she noticed, and took great care in examining award-winning pieces.

Each booth displayed a wide variety of goods. Not all vendors carried jewelry. Others offered pottery, artifacts, T-shirts, hats, craft supplies and books.

Tyler and Miles, snacking on beef jerky, trailed their dad as Annie wandered over to a lavishly decorated booth that caught her eye. Bold masks and delicately woven dream catchers were displayed above a porcelain doll collection.

Jamie pointed with a pudgy, brown finger. "They pretty, Mommy.

Annie moved forward. "Yes, they are."

Each skillfully painted doll wore a traditional outfit constructed from doeskin, feathers and tiny glass beads. The baby girl in the cradle board, she thought, was by the far the most beautiful. Laced into the animal-skin-covered board, the doll's round face peeked out from the opening. A golden complexion and dark eyes fringed in soft, curling lashes gave her a lifelike quality. A delicate smile touched her lips and rosy circles colored her cheeks.

Annie stood mesmerized. The doll looked a lot like the baby she had been daydreaming about—the child she imagined having with Dakota. Only the eyes were different, darker than she had envisioned.

"Do you like the baby?" A female voice asked.

Annie looked up, then down. The small-boned woman who had spoken stood well under five feet, her gray hair twisted into a topknot. Her skin, darkened by an indigenous heritage and possibly years in the sun, sported a road map of lines. A royal-blue dress decorated with multicolored ribbons flowed to her ankles. She appeared frail yet strong.

"Me like baby," Jamie said.

The old woman flashed a gap-toothed grin. "The baby looks like you, little one."

Annie shifted her son. The doll did resemble Jamie, but then so did Annie's daydream baby. "It's adorable. Did you make it?"

"Yes, they're all mine." She motioned to the dolls with pride, her eyes twinkling like a grandmother showing off her brood. "My name is Louisa Bright Flower."

"Hello. I'm Annie Graywolf and this is Jamie."

"Your boy's sweet."

"Thank you. I have two more."

"We have two more," a strong, masculine voice said behind her. "They're at the next booth looking at coloring books."

Annie turned, her knees weakening. Dakota's presence still made her heart flutter and limbs watery. "Louisa Bright Flower, this is my husband, Dakota."

The old woman studied him through catlike eyes: exotic, sharp and observant. "I know you." Tilting her head, she gave him another long, direct stare. "Yes, I know you well."

Although he smiled, his hands twitched, a clear sign that Louisa's tight scrutiny had him feeling like a specimen under a microscope. "I was a rodeo cowboy. A bull rider," he said. "People often think that I'm familiar, that they've met me before."

The gray-haired lady waved her bony hand. "Your being a cowboy isn't why I know you. It's more than that. You and I share the same medicine, the same spirit animal."

"The Lynx." Like a man being drawn into a hypnotic state, Dakota stepped forward, his eyes set on Louisa's. "Tell me what else you see."

"What you should be seeing." She took his hand, gazed at it for a long moment. "The Lynx knows things, his mind fills with mental pictures, but yours are blocked. You won't allow yourself to see what's there, to read others like you should."

She released his hand and reached for Annie's, gave it a pat, then stepped back. "Look at your wife and tell me what you see."

Dakota turned to Annie and smiled. A boyish, almost nervous smile. "A beautiful woman."

"And if you could give her an animal protector, what would it be?"

He answered hastily, his smile fading. "I don't know. I don't have the power to do that."

"Yes you do." Louisa clucked her tongue as if to reprimand his lack of spiritual confidence. "Look deep, Dakota. Into her soul. The protector is there."

Annie stood very still, her pulse hammering. She wasn't sure if she wanted Dakota to know her this way, to peel away the layers of her heart and enter her soul. Each time they made love, she felt closer to him. Too close. Annie feared she was falling in love with her husband, even though she was doing her best not to let it happen. She didn't want to be in love, not with a man whose apparent perfection could turn at any moment. Dakota wasn't a family man by nature.

"I can't see anything" he said finally to Louisa. "I just don't know."

The old woman shook her head. "Yes, you do. It's in her look, her touch, her scent. And you see it as well as feel it."

He closed his eyes, opened them, closed them again as though gaining the strength to speak. "Woman medicine. Female energy."

"And what animal provides woman medicine?"

He opened his eyes, gazed at Annie. "Otter."

Louisa continued the lesson in a patient tone. "And what are Otter's gifts?"

"Beauty and balance." He shifted his gaze from Annie to the child in her arms. "And motherhood. They care well for their young."

Apparently satisfied, the lines around Louisa's mouth softened into a smile. She reached out and touched Annie's shoulder. "This Otter needs many young. Babies fill her soul."

Annie silenced the catch in her throat. Dakota had just discovered, through a spiritual awakening of sorts, that she had been daydreaming about having more children.

Dakota trapped her gaze, and with it, her thundering heart. His eyes clouded with a mix of what seemed like wonder, curiosity and confusion.

Although he'd forgone using protection on their first night together, he'd used it every night since. Enough time had passed that Annie knew she hadn't become pregnant from their "honeymoon." A part of her wished she had. The thought scared her, just as the possibility of falling in love with Dakota did.

They stood staring at each other—a gaze more uncomfortable than any they had ever shared. Had he just read her mind? she wondered. Did he recognize her inner struggle? Did he know she was fighting her feelings?

Luckily Jamie's tiny voice broke through the silence that followed. "Baby," he said, pointing to the cradle board doll.

Dakota expelled a relieved breath. "How much is the doll?"

Louisa glanced at the porcelain figure. "Two hundred."

Dakota reached for his wallet, his tone respectful, if not humble. "I'll take it, but I'll give you a hundred more."

Annie understood why he had offered the extra money. It was payment for the reading. Whether or not the information had pleased him, it was the proper thing to do, and he was a man who adhered to Native American protocol. In the old days a blanket or other gift would have been given to a medicine woman for her service.

Annie waited quietly, certain Louisa would accept the generous offering. To refuse would dishonor Dakota.

The old lady removed the doll from the display case. "I'll box it up for you."

While Louisa stepped away to pack the doll, Dakota took Jamie from Annie and cuddled the child in his arms. "You wanted the one in the cradle board, right?"

She nodded. "Yes. Thank you."

Was the doll his way of giving her a baby? Did it hold significance, or was it simply an inanimate object? A gift without heartstrings attached? Regardless, Annie would cherish the cradle board baby forever.

Dakota tapped a booted foot. "I think I should check on the boys and get Jamie a coloring book, too. I'll be back in a minute."

"Okay." Annie watched him leave, Jamie peering over his shoulder.

When Louisa returned, Dakota was gone. Handing Annie the box, she spoke softly. "Although Lynx is the keeper of secrets, your husband has confused his medicine. Rather than keep his own secrets, he should be learning to sense the hidden thoughts and needs of those around him."

As a ray of sunlight caught Louisa's earrings, they glittered against her cheek. "And you, little Otter, are struggling with your medicine as well. Your constant worry upsets its balance. Woman energy is acceptance and trust."

She's right, Annie thought. *I worry about losing my husband.* It wasn't women like Sheila Harris that concerned her anymore; it was Dakota's need for emotional freedom. Love might stifle a man like him. "I'm trying to come to terms with it."

The older lady smiled. "I know. And I also know that the children you're raising aren't from Dakota's seed or your womb, but they belong to both of you just the same. They're what brought you together."

Tears formed in Annie's eyes. Louisa Bright Flower was a magical woman, a bright flower indeed.

Two hours later Annie and her family lounged in the picnic area, eating fry bread tacos. The boys sat on their own blanket, coloring pictures while they ate. Annie watched them, Louisa's words echoing in her mind.

Dakota tore off a piece of fry bread and stuffed it into his mouth. He had gone back to Louisa's booth and introduced her to Tyler and Miles, but hadn't mentioned her reading or what it had meant. Annie thought the experience had rattled him a little, that in his usual secretive way, he preferred not to explore their relationship by analyzing it too deeply. But the wise old woman had planted a seed of knowledge between them. They could either nourish it or keep it from taking root.

"Do you want to hear about my business plan?" Dakota asked.

Annie sat up a little straighter. Had her husband finally decided to share his thoughts and feelings, his hopes and dreams? Would this be the beginning of a new relationship for them? "Yes, please. Tell me everything."

He wiped his hands on a paper napkin, then brushed the bread crumbs from his lap. "I've decided to open a retail store. But not just your typical Western store. I want to carry handmade items, special merchandise." He glanced over at the boys, then back again. "That's why I've been collecting information about some of the craftspeople here. I'd like to give them a chance to sell their work in another realm, to promote their names in the Western market.''

Excitement bubbled in Annie's chest. This was something in which she could offer help, get involved. "I think it's a wonderful idea.''

His grin matched her joy. "Thanks. I know that my jewelry's good and it's selling fairly easily now, but that's mainly because of my background with the rodeo. And somehow that doesn't feel right. I'd rather promote other artists." He sipped his soda and continued. "My jewelry designs are personal to me. They've been a part of my healing, and that's how I would prefer to keep them. I'd be happy just making pieces for you.''

And she'd be happy to accept them, be part of his healing. She glanced at her wedding band. "Your work is personal to me, too. Very special.''

The warmth in his smile touched her like an intimate embrace. They gazed at each other, suddenly lost in the beauty around them: the aroma of food scenting the air, the green of the grass, blue of the sky. Their children just a few feet away.

He blinked first, breaking the contact. "I'm glad you approve.''

She approved of him, of the light dancing in his eyes. "You plan on carrying clothes, too. Right?''

"Yeah. All kinds of Western shirts. Vintage, handmade, simple, fancy. Same with boots and hats." He drew his knees up. "Now you can see why I'd be traveling quite a bit. Besides going to powwows to check out the talent there, I'd be hitting flea markets and swap meets. I can hire someone to manage the place, but I want to find most of the merchandise myself, especially the vintage and pawn pieces. And I'd like to develop a personal relationship with the silversmiths and clothing designers.''

She didn't want to think about his traveling. She preferred to think of the store as his home base, another reason, besides the children, for him to breeze back into town. "I'll help you however I can.''

"I was counting on that. You're part of the reason I came up with this idea. You've made your shop a success. Now I'd

like to try my luck. Hell, maybe I'll open locations all over
the States. Lord knows, I've been everywhere.''

Apparently financing this project wasn't an issue in his eyes.
Dakota was certainly astute enough to know how much capital
it would take. He must have saved quite a bit from his bull
riding days. Well, at least those days were over, she thought.
Her husband would own a place equipped with duds fit for the
flashiest rodeo cowboy, but thank God he wouldn't be one of
them.

Twelve

Dakota climbed into bed beside his wife. "The kids had fun, didn't they?"

She nodded. "So did I. I've always enjoyed powwows."

"Yeah, me, too." But he hadn't enjoyed being scrutinized by Louisa Bright Flower. He respected the older woman and her gift for reading someone's psyche, he just didn't like the idea that the mind she'd tapped into had been his.

His guilty mind, he thought. Dakota had the feeling Louisa knew he was keeping secrets from Annie. The whole experience had left him shaken—guilty and confused. Being caught by a medicine woman was a humbling experience.

And then there was all that talk about babies. He glanced at the cradle board doll Annie had placed on the dresser. Louisa had told him in no uncertain terms that Annie wanted more children.

They couldn't have a baby, could they? Somehow that would seem like too much of a commitment. Adopting the boys and marrying Annie was different. That was his duty as

Jill's brother. Dakota stole another glance at the doll. Not that he didn't like being a father. He loved the boys with all his heart. He couldn't imagine life without them.

What would it be like to have a daughter? he wondered, as he studied the doll's sweet face. A baby girl.

He shook the thought away as Annie reached out to him. "What are you thinking about?" she asked.

"Nothing." He toyed with the lace on her nightgown. She was naked underneath. Beautiful Annie. His wife. His lover.

No, he couldn't tell her about his secrets, not yet. He couldn't bear to jeopardize nights like this. Another month wouldn't make a difference. If anything, it would give him time to work on his approach. Dakota wasn't ready to cut open his soul. Admitting that the accident had left him emotionally scarred wasn't an easy thing to do.

Annie moved closer, brushing her nipples against his chest. He slipped the strap of her gown down to take one into his mouth. She mewled like a little kitten as he suckled.

Dakota felt himself harden as Annie slid her hand down his stomach, catching the waistband of his boxers. Without speaking, they shed their clothes and came together in an intimate embrace.

He stroked her between her thighs. She moved against his hand, wet and ready.

"I'll never get enough of you," he whispered as she arched and purred.

He reached for the condoms he kept in the dresser and tried not think about the baby they could create. He had already taken a risk their first time. He couldn't chance it again.

She parted her thighs to accept his penetration and he moved, slow and easy, slipping into her heat. They kissed with the tips of their tongues, then thrust deeper, mimicking the movement of their hips.

It was like making love on water, he thought, a warm, sexy wave. She climaxed first, urging his release. Dakota flung back his head as his body shuddered, the baby Annie wanted nothing more than a passing memory.

* * *

Annie looked up at her husband. Today Dakota had stopped by Intimate Silk after a business meeting. He had been scouting potential locations for the retail store he intended to open. A month had passed since he'd told Annie about his venture. She'd been working diligently beside him whenever possible, preparing the business plan. Being a wife, helpmate, mother and career woman suited all her needs. Annie had never been happier.

Dakota grinned. "How come you don't sell those edible undies?"

She gaped at him, then glanced quickly at her salesgirl who stood behind the counter, less than four feet away.

"*Dakota.* Don't say things like that."

"Why not?"

"Because Elaine will hear you."

"So. She's an adult. And she works in a lingerie boutique. I'm sure she's heard of edible undies."

"Shhh." Annie attempted to hush Dakota again. Thank goodness there weren't any customers in the store. "Behave yourself."

He persisted with a devilish grin. When Dakota wanted something, there was no stopping him. "What are they made out of, anyway?"

Annie glanced at Elaine again. Although the college student appeared completely engaged in rearranging the accessory shelves, an amused smile quivered her lips. Apparently she had tuned in to the "undies" conversation.

"Licorice," Annie said, answering Dakota's question. "At least, I think so." She didn't design candy panties.

His grin widened. "The red or black kind?"

She shook her head, laughing a little. "Dakota, knock it off."

He stepped closer. Dressed in one of his vintage shirts, he could have doubled for a rugged fashion model. Cowboy chic. The man definitely had taste.

He took her hand. "Let's go to the back room for a minute."

Annie shivered. His touch spread through her like warm

butter on freshly baked bread. Sweet and steamy. Heat flooded her loins. "Okay."

She knew the moment he closed the stockroom door behind them, that he would kiss her. Parting her lips, she welcomed his tongue, his taste, his texture. Life was good, Annie thought. She fretted less about being in love, and Dakota hadn't traveled nearly as much as she had expected. Regardless, their lovemaking sessions were always wilder upon his return, making them both anxious for the reunion.

"I want you," he groaned against her hair.

Her knees weakened. "Here? Now? We can't."

"I know, but every time I come into this store, I get turned on. All this satin and lace. Garter belts and silk stockings." He sucked her earlobe into his mouth. "There should be a law against designers like you."

Annie wound her arms around his neck. She wanted him, too. Wanted to pull his shirt open and graze his nipples with her teeth. Lick his navel. Kiss his… "Meet me here at closing time."

"Damn. You mean it?"

"Would I tease you about something as important as your sex drive?"

"Mine, huh? What about yours? If you were any hotter, the building would burst into flames."

Annie giggled. "Hmm. That might not be so bad. Some of those firefighters are pretty cute. Actually, I think there might even be a calendar in my desk somewhere."

"Well, get rid of it. I'm the only stud you're allowed to look at." He swept her into a hard, possessive kiss. "Remember, you're a married woman."

"A happy one," she whispered back.

"Yeah?"

"Yeah."

They separated and smiled at each other. "I wish I could take you to lunch, but I have another appointment," he said.

"That's okay. Maddie's coming in. I'm designing some pieces for her."

"Maddie?"

"The tall redhead who bought your bracelet."

"Oh, yeah. Your richest customer." Dakota brushed her cheek with a quick kiss. "I better go. I'll see you later."

"Closing time," she reminded him.

"Yeah." He sent her a roguish grin. "Closing time."

Thirty minutes later Maddie Ferguson breezed through the door and made a beeline for the champagne. "Hello, sugar." She poured herself a glass and smiled.

"Hi, Maddie. I've been working on some sketches for you."

"Great. Remember everything has to be red silk. My new boyfriend has this thing for red." She fluffed her hair. "All shades."

Annie nodded, realizing she'd have to put a rush on Maddie's order. The woman changed boyfriends as often as most people changed their socks. Her next lover might not be partial to red silk.

"Jerry's a cowboy," Maddie said, sipping her champagne. "He trains cutting horses. And he's a rodeo fan. He's been pestering me to introduce him to your husband." She cocked her head. "Speaking of which, you must be proud of that man of yours, getting back on that bull again. Jerry was really surprised. He thought that Dakota had retired for good."

Annie went still. Very still. "Dakota isn't…hasn't…he is retired…"

A nervous flush reddened the other woman's cheeks. "Oh, goodness, sugar. I guess I shouldn't have said anything, but I had no idea that you…"

Annie's stomach clenched. "Please. Just start from the beginning and tell me what you've heard."

Maddie set her champagne aside. "Jerry has a friend who works for Outlaw Boots as sales rep, someone named Wayne. Anyway, Wayne told Jerry that Outlaw Boots is endorsing Dakota in a special event. That he's agreed to ride that same bull again, and if he's successful, Outlaw will pay him an undisclosed amount of money." She widened her eyes. "A huge amount, from what Jerry gathered."

Annie gripped the bar as the room spun by in a sea of colors.

Dakota was returning to the rodeo? To ride Excalibur? The bull that had trampled him? "I can't believe it."

"From what Jerry was told, Outlaw has already started on the ad campaign. It's a big deal because that bull has never been ridden. And since Dakota has a personal stake in this, word is he's the cowboy to do it."

Annie knew all about Excalibur. That bull had thrown all of its previous riders, including Dakota, before the required eight seconds.

Openly frustrated, Maddie twisted a diamond on her finger. "I feel so awful. Here I went and spoiled your husband's surprise."

Annie just stared at the other woman. Apparently Maddie thought she should be happy about this news, and that Dakota's secret was well intentioned. "Don't blame yourself," Annie responded, struggling to keep her voice steady. "You didn't know."

"But still, I should have kept my big mouth shut. I'm so sorry, sugar."

Not half as sorry as I am, Annie thought, her throat constricting. *I'm the one who fell in love with a man I can never trust.*

Intimate Silk was closed, the register cashed out, the doors locked. Annie and Dakota should have been making love in the stockroom, touching and kissing. Instead they faced each other on the sales floor, Dakota's deception hovering over them like a dark cloud.

He stood against the front counter, his white shirt with its shimmering silver trim a stark contrast to the vacant look in his black eyes, grim line of his lips, stern set of his jaw.

As Annie backed into a display rack, one of the chrome bars jabbed her spine. "Then it's true?" she asked.

He responded with a tight nod.

Her voice vibrated. "How could you do this to me? Do you know how I felt, being told something like that from a customer?" Somehow she had managed to get through the rest of the day without breaking down into shoulder-racking sobs.

Her pride had wrapped itself so tightly around her heart she couldn't find the emotional strength to cry.

"I'm sorry." Dakota exhaled audibly. "I planned on telling—"

"When?" she shot back, feeling suddenly viperous, her tone laced with poison. "From what I understand, an advertising campaign is already underway. You must have secured this deal a while ago. And here I'd thought that you'd been forced to retire. That you couldn't go back." She narrowed her eyes, hating him. Loving him. Hating that she loved him. "Is it the money? Is that what's driving you to do this?"

He shook his head. "The money doesn't matter. I'd ride Excalibur for free."

Although Annie hugged herself, the gesture lacked comfort. She loved him. And because she loved him, she couldn't stand by and watch him teeter on the edge, endanger injuries that barely had time to heal. "What if you get hurt again?"

"I won't."

Tears stung the back of her eyes, tears that refused to fall. "You could, Dakota. You know you could. There's no guarantee that what happened last time won't happen again." And there was no guarantee that he wouldn't end up like her father.

His jaw twitched. "Then that's a chance I'll have to take."

Oh, God. She rocked forward. "I don't understand."

He swallowed and expelled a heavy breath. "I've been anxiety-ridden ever since my accident, Annie. I panicked when I landed beneath the bull. I was literally paralyzed with fear. And I've been reliving that moment almost every day since." He lifted his chin. "I don't want to see that image of myself for the rest of my life. Please, squirt, I'm asking you to support my decision."

"I can't." She shook her head. How could he ask for her support when he knew her own father had been killed by a bull? "You know how much I hate the rodeo. It reminds me of my dad." Of everything bad that had happened in her life.

He blew a frustrated breath. "I'm not your father. I'm not drinking my life away and taking stupid chances. This is different."

Not to Annie it wasn't. "Where does this leave us, Dakota?"

"Nowhere, I guess, if you don't try to understand."

What's to understand? He'd been lying all along. "Is that some sort of ultimatum?"

He pulled a hand through his hair, his voice taking on a bite. "Yeah, maybe it is."

"Oh, I get it." Allowing her anger to blind the hurt, she set her jaw. "I'm supposed to be a dutiful little wife and let my man do whatever he wants. Give him carte blanche to play cowboy, be wild and free whenever the mood strikes. Well, that doesn't work for me." And because it didn't, she knew he'd always feel the need to keep secrets.

"Damn it." When he lifted his foot, his heel caught the base of the counter, rattling the glass. "I already told you, this isn't about looking for some excitement in my life. It goes deeper than that." Once again he tugged a hand through his hair, rearranging the already tousled layers. "I was defeated, Annie. If I don't at least try to ride Excalibur, then I've let that bull beat me."

She crossed her arms. The rodeo wasn't a battle. He wasn't a warrior counting coup for his honor. He was a man taking an unnecessary chance. "But you've already fought back. You beat the odds. You walked again. That should be enough."

He stared her down, his dark gaze boring into hers. "Well, it's not."

Suddenly at an impasse, they both fell silent. And in the stillness, surrounded by the femininity of her store, Annie realized how out of place he was. In her life and in her heart. He wasn't the kind of man she should have fallen in love with, yet she had. And even though she would probably never stop loving him, she couldn't accept his reckless nature or his lies.

Numb, she uncrossed her arms and let them fall. She felt lifeless, like a rag doll. Not flesh and bone, but fabric and thread, lacking human warmth and vitality. "What about the kids?"

Confusion flashed across his face. "What about them?"

"What do we tell them...about us?"

"Nothing." Dakota looked as inhuman as she felt. He stood like a statue—a tall, cold form carved of stone. "We're still married, Annie."

Until the adoption is finalized, she thought. He'd be there for the kids, but not for her. Eventually he would leave, and they'd become a statistic. A single mother and a weekend dad. Divorced parents of three.

She found her voice, shaky though it was. "Don't you think the boys are going to sense there's something wrong?"

"We can't let them," he responded. "They deserve some security in their lives. You and I will just have to pretend."

With that said, Dakota straightened his shoulders and strode toward the glass door. He turned the key planted in the lock and disappeared into the dusk. A few moments later Annie relocked the door, then burst into tears.

"Daddy!"

Dakota heard Jamie calling him from the bathroom the boys used. The kids bathed every night, and since Jamie required assistance, Dakota and Annie shared the responsibility.

Dakota released a heavy breath. He had done his damnedest to act normal around the kids and so had Annie. Neither had said more than two words to each other over dinner, but the boys hadn't paid much attention. Dakota had suggested dining in front of the TV, hoping to use it as a shield.

Annie had come home late, so Dakota had relieved the housekeeper and started the meal on his own. When Annie finally did walk through the door, her swollen eyes and pink nose indicated a crying jag. She had done a clever job of concealing most of it with makeup and possibly some eye drops, but he knew her features too well not to have noticed. Besides, tears were expected. They had practically ended their marriage tonight. In a sense they had. Not legally, but emotionally.

Dakota pasted a phony smile on his face and entered the bathroom. Jamie, pushing a plastic boat through a haze of bubbles, grinned up at him.

Annie knelt beside the tub, washcloth in hand, platinum hair spilling down her back in soft, luxurious waves. Dakota's chest tightened, hoping she wouldn't turn around and catch him staring at her.

"Play, Daddy," Jamie said, offering the boat clutched in his tiny hand.

Dakota stepped forward and knelt beside Annie without glancing her way. He accepted the yellow boat and winked at his son.

"Looks like you've got extra bubbles tonight," he said, shifting his gaze to the plastic bottle perched on the side of the tub. The animated container brought back a flood of childhood memories. He reached for it, crossing Annie's path. She pulled back, away from his extended arm. "I used to use this stuff, too," he remarked, struggling to fill the awkward silence.

Jamie removed a mesh net from the shower caddy and dumped half of its contents into the water. Dakota knelt there, watching him, the bubble bath in one hand, the plastic boat in the other. Annie's presence was too vivid to ignore. He could see her in his peripheral vision, smell the floral scent of her perfume. Damn, he ached to touch her, to apologize for making her cry. But what good would it do? He couldn't apologize for his decision to ride Excalibur. That would be like apologizing for who he was, for who he'd ever been.

Annie leaned forward. "Jamie, it's time to wash."

The boy wrinkled his nose, but allowed his mother to clean his face. Dakota studied her hands, already missing her delicate touch upon his own skin.

"Mommy, kiss," Jamie said, as she scrubbed his back with the washcloth.

Annie puckered, and Jamie smacked her lips with a loud smooch, grabbing her face with wet, soapy hands. The child's fingers marked the front of her hair with a cluster of white bubbles.

They both giggled, making Dakota feel like an outsider. Would she ask him to leave once the adoption was final? Would she apologize to Harold and tell him that she had tried to make the marriage work, but Dakota was the wrong man for her?

He studied Annie's profile, the feminine arch of her eyebrow, curling lashes, full, lush lips. The thought of her finding someone else someday formed a tight knot right in the center of his gut.

"Can Daddy have a hug?" he asked Jamie.

Jamie squealed and lunged for Dakota. Dakota caught the child's slippery body and held him. The boy's tiny heartbeats thudded against his own.

Jamie squirmed out of his father's arms, leaving Dakota's T-shirt with a damp impression. "Hug Mommy now."

"Sure, go ahead."

"No, you hug Mommy," the child replied.

"Me?" Dakota nearly tripped over his tongue. Turning toward Annie, he searched her face for approval, for a change of heart. Their eyes met and held, and for one brief moment a ray of hope glimmered. But only for a moment. Quickly Annie glanced down at the floor as though meeting his gaze had burned her eyes.

Dakota turned away. Damn it. Didn't she know how much he needed her?

"Hug," Jamie said again.

Dakota winced. Jamie might be too young to comprehend the enormity of the situation, but he wasn't too young to sense the change in his parents' behavior. Normally Annie and Dakota flicked bubbles at each other during Jamie's bath, making the boy laugh and join in.

Dakota struggled for an excuse to keep his hands off his wife. "I'll get Mommy all wet," he said finally, indicating the damp spot on his shirt.

"Then Mommy hug Daddy."

Even through his agony, Dakota couldn't help but laugh. Jamie had an insistent, if not stubborn, personality. "She'll still get wet, slugger."

The boy turned to Annie. "You no want to get wet?"

"No, sweetheart. Not tonight." Her voice sounded sad. Frail and broken.

Dakota sighed. If she needed him, too, then why wasn't she willing to accept his decision? Be a supportive wife? It wasn't fair that she kept comparing him to her father.

He glanced over at Jamie. Like most small children, the boy's attention span had faltered. Jamie dismantled a toy submarine, the nonexistent hug forgotten.

An hour later the boys rested in their beds, sleepy dogs in tow. Dakota loaded the dishwasher, giving Annie time alone in their bedroom. When he finally entered the room, he found her lying on her side of the bed, the blanket pulled tight.

"Am I allowed to join you?"

"Of course you are. The kids would get suspicious if one of us started sleeping on the couch."

Her voice was as rigid as her spine, making him wonder where the fragile woman in the bathroom had gone. Was she angry that he hadn't hugged her? No. That wasn't possible. If she longed for his touch, she would have reached out to him.

He tore off his shirt and tossed it into the hamper. "I guess I should increase my traveling schedule. That way I won't occupy your bed. At least not very often."

She tugged the blanket tighter. "Whatever. Your life is your own, Dakota. Live it the way you want."

"Fine. I will," he snapped back, pulling his jeans down.

Dakota discarded his pants and moved toward the bed. He'd go away as often as he could. And while he was gone, he'd sleep in dark, lonely motel rooms and miss the hell out of the woman who no longer wanted to be his wife.

Sometime later Dakota fell into a restless sleep only to be awakened by muffled sounds. Soft feminine cries.

He turned toward Annie's side of the bed and pushed the blanket away. Her place was empty. Dakota sat up and rubbed his eyes. Light spilled from beneath the master-bathroom door. He landed on his feet and followed the pale glow.

"Annie?" he called her name and tried the door.

She sat upon the tiled floor, hugging herself. With her hair cascading over her shoulders and her body draped in a pale-pink nightgown, she looked delicate, he thought, like a tiny, glass figurine.

He knelt in front of her and lifted her chin. Red-rimmed eyes stared back at him. "I never cry," she said. "Or at least I haven't in a long time."

Dakota brushed his hand across her cheek, collecting her tears. "Then I guess you're due." She'd been due earlier, too, he supposed. Her husband had lied to her. A lie of omission, but a lie just the same. "I'm sorry. I should have told you right away, but I was convinced once we became lovers that you'd understand. That we'd be close enough for both of us to handle this."

It had been difficult for him to admit his fears to the woman he had vowed to protect. Warriors weren't supposed to panic. And if they did, they shouldn't advertise their weakness to their wives. It was a man's place to remain strong.

She sniffed. "I keep thinking about my dad."

"I know, baby. But what I'm doing has nothing to do with him." He searched for an analogy to make her understand. "If your dad and I were airline pilots and he was killed on the job, would you expect me to quit flying? Or let's say that I had developed a fear of flying, wouldn't you want me to overcome it? Don't you think that's what a man should do?"

"But bull riding is different. It's not like other jobs. It's not necessary for you to go back."

"It is to me," he responded quietly.

Annie sniffed again, and he gave in to the urge to hold her, cradle her in his arms. When he reached out, she fell into his embrace, her tears moistening his bare shoulder.

He stroked her hair while she cried, knowing it was the only comfort he had to give. He didn't understand her any more than she understood him.

"I think I should probably get on the road tomorrow. I think it would be easier on both of us," he said, hardly recognizing the rough, tortured sound of his own voice.

The adoption was nearly final, but Dakota didn't have the heart to tell Harold how upset Annie was. He had been confiding in Harold, and the older man seemed certain that his decision to ride Excalibur wouldn't interfere with the marriage. But it had.

Dakota had vowed to be good husband, yet he was losing his wife. Possibly losing her forever.

Thirteen

Marilyn Monroe was a beauty, but keeping a white horse clean wasn't an easy task. Annie, dressed in her grubbiest clothes, stood beside the cross-tied mare. Lifting a sponge from the bucket, she lathered a small section of Marilyn's damp coat. As Annie worked, she couldn't help but smile. Marilyn, the blue-eyed equine, enjoyed being pampered. Each time Marilyn batted her baby blues, Annie was half tempted to paint the preening mare's hoofs with a sparkling coat of ruby-red nail polish.

"I miss Dakota," she told the horse. Annie had seen her husband exactly six times in the past two months. And on each of those occasions, Dakota had slept in Jamie's room and showered in the bathroom the boys used. Although some of his clothes still occupied her closet and his ring still rested on her finger, she didn't feel much like a married woman. What she felt was devastated.

Annie rinsed the lathered section on Marilyn's coat and went on to soap the next. The horse whinnied her approval. Marilyn had become a trusted friend. The horse always seemed to listen with a sympathetic, nonjudgmental ear.

"I wonder if I should wash my hair with your shampoo," she mused aloud to the horse while sponging on the blue liquid. "It's not likely Dakota will ever make another bottle for me."

Annie lifted the hose and sprayed Marilyn's back. Yes, she missed Dakota. Missed laughing and loving with him. Missed his rakish smile and onyx eyes, his messy hair, fancy vintage shirts and time-worn boots. That big bathtub and even bigger bed weren't nearly as inviting without him.

An hour later Marilyn glowed and Annie's arms ached. She leaned against the barn wall and peered around the corner as footsteps approached. Six of them. Two belonged to Tyler and the other four to Dog Soldier, his ever-faithful companion.

"Hi, Tyler. I just gave Marilyn a bath. What do you think?"

The boy studied the horse from beneath his glasses, his brown eyes soft and soulful. "She looks pretty. Does she have to stand like that until she's dry?"

"It won't hurt her to stay cross tied for a little while." Annie, nearly as wet as Marilyn, needed to dry in the sun, as well. "I could walk her I suppose, but I'm beat."

Tyler stroked the mare's nose. The horse nuzzled in response. "Uncle Kody just called."

Annie's heart skipped a beat. "He did?" *Did he ask for me? No,* she thought. *He had called to talk to his kids, not the wife he'd rejected.* "So, what did he have to say?"

"He'll be here on Thursday."

She swallowed the lump in her throat. "To take you boys to the rodeo." Dakota's rodeo. His showdown with Excalibur.

"Uh-huh." Tyler continued to reward the appreciative mare with gentle strokes. "Are you guys still mad at each other?"

Oh, good heavens. Sweet, sensitive Tyler. Pretending in front of him was impossible. And she and Dakota hadn't done the best job. Each time they saw each other made the next that much harder.

"Your father and I aren't mad." Hurt. They were hurt. Two people who didn't understand each other.

"How come he always sleeps in Jamie's room when he comes home?"

Annie sighed. Making excuses to Tyler pained her, but explaining something she barely comprehended herself was clearly impossible. "You know how much Jamie misses his dad. I think he stays with Jamie to make up for his being gone so much."

Tyler stepped away from the mare and sat down in the dirt beside Dog Soldier. The dog panted happily. "But you miss Uncle Kody, too."

As Annie lowered herself to the ground, her damp jeans formed cakes of mud. "You're right, I do. But I'm an adult, and I understand that his work takes him out of town."

The boy furrowed his brow. "You're not going to the rodeo, are you?"

"No." She couldn't bear to watch Dakota ride that bull. She had avoided rodeos since her father died. But what hurt just as badly was Dakota's deception. He had lured Outlaw Boots, not the other way around. Before Dakota had contacted his former sponsor, they, like everyone else, hadn't known he was willing or able to return to the rodeo.

Tyler sat with his head held high and legs crossed Indian style. "I wish you were coming with us."

Annie's heart clenched. Her son looked so grown up, so proud, like a young Cheyenne brave. "I'm sorry. I just can't."

"But Uncle Kody loves you."

"Did he say that over the phone?"

"No, but I'm sure he does."

Annie gazed around. Everything reminded her of Dakota: the barn he had ordered, the horses he'd bought, cattle he'd roped, ground he'd walked upon, flowers he'd planted. She loved him desperately, yet she couldn't ignore the fact that he hadn't fallen in love with her.

"Come on." She rose to her feet. "Why don't we take Marilyn for that walk. She looks a little bored."

"Okay." Tyler reached for his mother's hand.

Her skin warmed from his touch. She kissed the top of his head and silently thanked God for her children.

"Uncle Kody's here!"

Miles tore out the front door, leaving Annie alone in the

kitchen, holding a large serving tray. She exhaled a shaky breath and gripped the metal. Dakota was early. They hadn't expected him until that evening.

She stood in the center of the kitchen, wondering if she should greet him, or go about her business until he approached her?

Choosing the latter, she carried the tray through the back door and placed it on the patio table. "Your dad's here," she told Tyler and Jamie.

Immediately they abandoned Jamie's inflatable pool and ran off to welcome Dakota, the family dogs nipping at their heels.

The unattended hose sprang free and poured water onto the grass. Annie anchored it, then returned to the table where she unloaded the tray, arranging hamburger buns, condiments and paper plates.

Moments later the dogs raced back into the yard as the merriment of her children's breathless chatter mingled with the click of Dakota's boots. Annie's smile belied the aching beats of her heart. Her husband stood on the patio, surrounded by his sons. The boys, each dressed in their swim trunks, clung possessively to the man they adored.

A warm breeze teased Dakota's hair. Annie noticed it hadn't been trimmed in months. The longer length strengthened his rebellious appeal. He wore a simple white T-shirt and jeans. He had that bad-boy look today. Untamed yet clean. She wondered if he missed smoking. He almost seemed out of place without a cigarette dangling from the corner of his lips.

Dakota's gaze slid over her. "So you're barbecuing."

Annie smoothed her cotton dress. Summer had passed, but the California sun remained. "We've been having a heat wave. It seemed like a good idea."

He nodded toward the grass. "Looks like the pool's overflowing."

Annie turned, grateful for an excuse to break eye contact. "Boys, shut the water off."

The three stumbled onto the lawn together, giggling and pushing. While they enjoyed the ill-fated reunion and splashed each other in the pool, Annie glanced up at Dakota. "You'll join us, won't you?"

He returned her overly polite invitation with a casual acceptance that seemed feigned. "Sure. Thanks. Can I help with anything?"

"That's not necessary. You're probably tired. You've had a long drive." Or she assumed he did. She had no idea where he'd traveled from or the last city in which he'd slept.

"I'm fine. And I'd like to help."

"All right."

She offered him the job of lighting the charcoal. As Dakota strode over to the barbecue, Annie returned to the kitchen. By the time she finished the salad preparations, hamburgers sizzled on the grill.

Annie stood beside the glass-top table, pouring lemonade into tall plastic tumblers. If anyone would have peeked over the fence, she thought, they would have viewed a lie—a happy, well-adjusted family barbecuing on a sunny afternoon. She hadn't meant to place herself in such an uncomfortable position. She hadn't anticipated Dakota's early arrival. Never would she have planned a picnic with his involvement. On previous visits, he had taken the kids out for pizza, falling easily into the routine of a weekend dad.

Dakota and Annie ate with their children, both adults visibly uncomfortable in the other's presence. Annie picked at her food, avoiding Dakota's piercing gaze whenever possible. It actually hurt to look at him, to see him looking back at her with those dark, indiscernible eyes.

When the last burger was gone, Tyler shuffled his brothers back to the inflatable pool where he orchestrated a battleship game with Jamie's plastic, neon boats. Although Tyler's ruse was subtle, Annie had caught on. The boy wanted to give his parents time alone, apparently hoping they'd talk and smile the way they used to.

Unable to deliberately thwart Tyler's heart-wrenching plan, Annie gazed across the table at her estranged husband and initiated polite conversation.

"How's the store coming?"

"All right, I guess. I'm still scouting locations. I'm thinking maybe Nashville or Santa Fe. I don't know."

She glanced over at the kids to catch Tyler watching. "They're both Western-orientated towns." Two months ago Dakota had intended to open the store in Old Town Temecula. Apparently that was no longer an option. "I guess you've been everywhere lately."

Dakota crumbled a potato chip. "Yeah. I even went home for a spell."

"Home?"

He raised his eyes to hers. "Montana. That's where I live, remember?"

Painful as it was, she held his stare. *I thought you lived here.* "Of course, your cabin." His rustic, mountain dwelling. "I'll bet it's getting chilly there now."

He dropped his gaze. "Uh-huh. Are the kids all packed for tomorrow?"

A dark cloud floated over her heart. How had two people who had loved and laughed turned into such strangers? The adoption had been finalized. The children belonged to her and Dakota now, even if their marriage had faltered. "They've been packed for days. They're really excited about this trip."

"That's understandable. They didn't get to go last time."

Last time undoubtedly meant Dakota and Annie's wedding. Of all places, Dakota's return to the rodeo had been scheduled in Las Vegas. "Is Mary meeting you at the airport?"

He went back to crushing potato chips. "Yeah. Haven't you talked to her?"

"I was just checking to see if any of the plans had changed." Mary, having done her best to remain neutral, would be there to support Dakota and watch the kids. Annie would be forever grateful.

"No. Nothing's changed," he responded. "Absolutely nothin'."

As their conversation ceased, the world closed in, heightening Annie's senses. The sun appeared brighter, the children's laughter louder, the burning-charcoal scent stronger. Unfortunately, everything about Dakota intensified, too. His hair looked messier, his cheekbones higher, his shoulders broader.

She gazed at his lips, at the fullness, and couldn't help but remember the masculine flavor of his last kiss.

She rose abruptly. "I guess I should get this mess cleaned up."

"I'll help." He replaced the cap on the ketchup bottle. "Hey, is that kid working out, the one I hired to look after the horses?"

"He's doing fine." But it wasn't the same as seeing her husband at the barn every morning, standing amid the dawn, freshly showered and ready to greet the day. The horses still whinnied for him.

Dakota loaded the tray with condiment jars and plastic containers. "Does Maria still work here?"

"Oh, yes." Annie gathered the soiled plates and explained the housekeeper's absence. "I gave her the next couple of days off. She's going to Mexico this weekend, and I thought she might appreciate an early start."

"I guess I should have called first, but I didn't expect to find you home at this hour. You know, on a Thursday."

"I left work early." The boys had attended school that day, so she'd picked up Jamie from preschool and made it home just in time to meet Tyler and Miles at the bus stop. For Annie the barbecue served as a late lunch; for the kids, an early dinner.

Dakota followed Annie into the kitchen. The counters, she noted, were littered with remnants from the salad fixings. She stacked the paper plates beside the mess and scanned the cabinet for large-size trash bags while Dakota returned condiment jars to the refrigerator. Locating the bags, she peeled one out of the box.

"Hey, squirt?"

She glanced up. "Hmm?"

"I like your dress. You look pretty in it."

Annie stilled. How she longed for the impossible, the fairy tale of happily-ever-after. "Thank you. It's not new, though. You've seen it before."

His husky voice took on a low, sensual quality—a near whisper. "I know."

Annie stood awkwardly then, clutching the trash bag. The floral-printed dress, she suddenly realized, was the one Dakota had stripped from her body the first time they had made love. Quickly she turned away and busied her quaking hands.

His voice sounded behind her. "Is there any chance you might change your mind and come to Vegas with us? It would be nice to have you there. You know, as a friend."

Annie's next breath clogged her throat. She wished so badly that he loved her, that he wanted to be her husband more than he wanted to ride that bull. "Dakota, I can't…"

"Well, just in case, I'll leave a rodeo ticket for you at the ticket booth. Maybe you'll see things differently by Saturday."

"I won't," she whispered, as he turned and walked out of the room. "I won't."

Friday night in Las Vegas. Dakota gazed out the hotel room window. The Strip blazed with life. Flashing lights and neon signs lit up the sky. Tourists strolled in and out of casinos, while buses, rental cars and cabs crowded the roads. Dakota enjoyed the glitz, the seasoned entertainers, the gambling, the free drinks and the rodeo fans. Vegas was his kind of town.

But not tonight. Tonight it reminded him of Annie and the chapel where they had taken their vows. Kissed for the first time. Made promises they hadn't kept.

He plowed his hands through his hair and turned away from the window. If ever there was a time he needed his wife, it was now, on the night before his return to the rodeo.

He looked around the room, feeling empty and alone. Outlaw Boots had rented him a two-bedroom suite, but he'd turned it over to Mary and the boys. And the only reason he hadn't stayed with them was because he'd been hoping his wife would show. But she hadn't.

He lifted the phone and dialed the suite. He needed to talk to the kids, hear their sweet little voices just one more time. His parents and Harold were due to arrive tomorrow. Everyone but Annie would be there.

Mary answered on the third ring, her tone gravelly. Dakota winced, hoping she wouldn't snarl at him. Since he could tell that he'd gotten her out of bed, he glanced at the clock and caught his blunder. It was later than he'd realized. "Hey, Sis. I guess there's no need to ask if the kids are still up."

"Hardly. They crashed hours ago." Her voice softened as she came more awake. "What's the matter, are you lonely?"

His sister knew him well, sometimes too well. "I'm all right," he answered, thinking he was beyond lonely. His missed his wife. Desperately. "So are you enjoying that suite?" he asked, changing the subject.

"Am I ever. You saw this place. It's gorgeous."

"Yeah." He studied his own room. Subdued, monochromatic furnishings boasted sophisticated elegance. Blond wood displayed cream-colored upholstery, and a pale satin comforter draped the bed. "Believe me, this isn't the way most cowboys live. I never stayed in digs like this when I rode the circuit, let alone been offered a suite like the one you're in."

"I know, I'm the daughter of a professional cowboy, remember? But as I recall, you did all right. Better than Dad. You landed some pretty sweet endorsement deals." Pride brightened her tone. "Of course, now you've graduated to a new level of fame. You're a headliner. A main event."

"I don't care about all that. That's not why I'm doing this."

"I know. I understand."

He stared at the walls, suddenly craving a drink, something to numb the pain. "I wish Annie did."

"You could call her."

"And tell her what? That tomorrow's victory will be empty without her?"

"Sounds like a good start to me."

Out of habit, Dakota pulled a hand through his hair. "I can't say that."

Mary sighed. "Why not?"

"Because…I just can't." Did his sister expect him to beg Annie for her support? His wife had made a choice she knew had wounded him. Was he supposed to go crawling back to her like a spineless pup licking those wounds?

No way, he thought.

"Seems to me there are a lot of things you have trouble saying."

Dakota narrowed his eyes, giving the phone a pointed stare. "What's that supposed to mean?"

"What do you think it means?" she retorted, her voice as sharp as his.

"Don't start, okay? I'm not in the mood." He knew what Mary's probing meant. His sister thought he was in love with Annie.

Anxious to drown his emotions in a drink, he grabbed his shirt off the bed. He would hit the casino, down a little whisky and play a little cards. He didn't need to have this conversation, didn't need the hurt it caused.

"Good night, Sis. I'm going downstairs for a while." Supporting the phone with his shoulder, Dakota tucked in his shirt, then zipped his jeans. "I'll come by in the morning to see the kids." He hung up before Mary could argue, ignoring her disapproving tsk.

Whisky, it seemed, had always served as his remedy for loneliness—a warm, gut-clenching drink. Did he really like the taste or was it the color that intrigued him? The amber fire? The intoxicating glow of a whisky-eyed woman?

Yes, it was the woman, he realized. The little blonde who had occupied his thoughts for years. *Years.* What kind of man would carry a sexual torch for over a decade?

One who was in love, his mind answered. What he felt for Annie went beyond sex.

At what precise moment his heart had tripped and stumbled, he couldn't say. But now he knew that he hadn't agreed to marry Annie out of duty. Sure, that's what he'd told himself— a stubborn cowboy refusing to acknowledge that he had loved her even then.

He glanced at the phone. Should he call Annie? Forget his pride and admit how much she meant to him? How much he needed her? Would it even matter to his wife?

Nothing had changed. Not really. He was still riding Excalibur tomorrow, something Annie didn't want him to do. Dakota reached for his wallet and shook off the notion to call, loneliness creeping in once again.

Fourteen

Annie stood in the hallway of the hotel, her heart hammering in time to her nerves.

She reached up to knock on room 516, but before her hand made the connection, the door flew open. Startled, she jumped back, then stood motionless, staring at the man she'd come to see.

Dakota's frame filled the doorway, his expression equally stunned. "Oh, my God, you're here."

Her stomach did an anxious flip. He wore a Western shirt and jeans, a tousled strand of ebony hair falling over his forehead. She resisted the urge to tame it. "Looks like you were on your way out."

"Yeah. I was just going to check out the casino." He searched her gaze. "Are you here to go to the rodeo tomorrow, or were you hoping to talk me out of it?"

"I..." She had come to support him, but part of her was still afraid to say it out loud. Once she did, there would be no turning back. She'd have to sit with the rest of the audience and watch him ride that bull, grip the rail and pray for his safety. "You said that you needed a friend." Not a wife, but a friend, she recalled.

"Yeah, I do." He stepped away from the door. "Come in, please."

She entered the room, then stood awkwardly, clutching the strap on her handbag. He hooked his thumbs into his front pockets, the gesture as self-protective as hers.

Annie chewed her lip. Should she tell him that she had cried at home? Stood before his side of the closet and touched the suit he'd worn on their wedding day? She had fingered the shirt and held the jacket against her face, grateful it hadn't been laundered. A trace of Dakota's scent had drifted to her nostrils—a subtle wisp of cologne and tobacco trapped in time.

And at that heart-clenching moment she had realized what she had been disclaiming all along. Her husband was as a warrior, a modern-day Cheyenne going into battle, a man who had the right to regain his honor.

Dakota motioned for her to sit, so she perched on the edge of the bed, hating how guarded they both seemed. She gazed around the room and noticed a tall bouquet of flowers on the table. They were bright and festive, almost out of place amid the subtle decor.

He followed her sight to the mixed bouquet. "They're from the hotel. Kind of a good-luck thing for tomorrow, I guess." He walked toward the arrangement, removed a daisy and handed it to her. "I wanted to send them back, but I knew I couldn't. The hotel staff wouldn't have understood."

She clutched the flower, comprehending his meaning. Daisies reminded him of the sunny kitchen she had decorated, the room in which they had shared family meals. "I don't know what to say." She wanted to say that she loved him, but knew now wasn't the time. She had come as a friend, not a woman trying to pressure a man or make him feel guilty for not returning her affection. If unrequited love was her fate, then she would accept it gracefully.

He leaned against the table and stared down at her, his expression indiscernible. "You could tell me why you're really here. I'm still not exactly clear if you're going to be at the rodeo or not."

Annie plucked a flower petal, then stopped herself instantly. "I'll be there, but I can't promise that I won't be nervous." She still had fears of him getting hurt, of losing him the way she had lost her father. As much as she tried to blind herself from that image, she couldn't make it go away.

Dakota sat beside her, his expression softening. "That's okay. I'll probably be nervous, too. In fact, I know I will. I've got a lot of anxiety wrapped up in this rodeo. Years of it."

She reached over and touched his hair, smoothing the strands on his forehead. "I know."

He scooted closer and placed his head against her shoulder. "Thanks for being here, Annie. I know this isn't easy for you. It isn't easy for either one of us."

For a long, silent moment, she held him, rocking gently. The yellow bloom fell from her lap and landed beside them. She glanced at its sunny form.

"When I was a little girl, I used to pretend that you were my boyfriend. And I'd play that silly flower game, too. 'He loves me, he loves me not.'" She could still see herself sitting in the middle of her mother's garden, a heap of torn petals at her feet.

Dakota lifted his head. "Maybe I should try that."

Annie reached for the daisy. "You don't need to."

He swallowed, his voice breaking a little. "Is that why you're really here, squirt? Because you love me?"

She nodded, her chest constricting. "Yes, but I know that you don't feel the same way about me, and I'm not asking you to." She couldn't force a man to love her. She knew better than that, and she loved him enough to give him the freedom he craved. Clipping Dakota's wings would be like gunning down a beautiful bird in flight. He had the right to seize his moment, face the rodeo and conquer it. "I'll be your friend, be there whenever you need me, but I would never pressure you to—"

"Shh." He placed his finger against her lips. "Don't say

any more. Just listen. I do love you, Annie. I have for years, only I didn't know it back then.''

She shook her head, disbelief clouding her emotions. "Has Mary been talking to you? Convincing you that you feel this way?''

"Yeah, she talked to me, but this has nothing to do with my sister. I agreed to marry you and adopt the kids two years ago. Harold approached me about it soon after my accident.''

Struggling to absorb his words, she only stared. "You agreed to marry me beforehand? Why didn't you tell me? Why did you act as if you didn't know?''

"Pride,'' he responded simply. "I didn't want to be the one to propose. I didn't want to be that vulnerable. And I didn't want you to know what I'd been through.'' He reached out to stroke her hair, his breath hitching. "After the accident, I couldn't, um—'' he paused for a moment, then went on "—I wasn't functioning sexually, and the doctors didn't have a clear-cut answer as to whether I ever would.''

Annie listened while he explained the medical reason behind his impotency, the damage that had been done to his spine, an injury that, luckily, wasn't beyond repair. "Even though it wasn't my fault, I still felt like less of a man. But once Harold approached me about marrying you, I knew I had to get better. It was a reason to go on, not to give up.''

She gazed up at him. "I'm the first woman you've made love to since your accident, aren't I?''

"I didn't want anyone but you. You've been a part of me for years. Only I thought it was just sexual attraction back then. I know better now.''

The tears fogging her eyes began to fall. "I was part of your recovery.'' A part of his soul, she realized, a part of who he was and ever would be. "Oh, Dakota, what you just told me means so much.'' It meant that he loved her. Truly loved her.

"I'll never let my pride get in the way of how I feel, not ever again. I need you, Annie.''

She needed him, too. For the rest of her life. "So you're going to come back to California and live with me?''

He nodded. "And I'm going to open that store in Old Town Temecula. I want to be wherever you and the kids are."

She smiled. His eyes were nearly as watery as hers, but he made no attempt to wipe away the moisture. They were crying together. "We can redecorate the house. Maybe pick out some furniture together." It would no longer be her house, she decided, it would theirs. She would add his name to the deed, welcome him in every way.

He brushed her lips in a tender kiss. "I don't think we should change the kitchen. I think it's perfect the way it is."

Annie deepened the kiss. "I love you," she whispered.

"I love you, too." He leaned in close and nuzzled her neck.

She all but melted from his touch. His skin was warm, his clean-shaven jaw smooth. She untucked his shirt and opened the buttons one by one.

They took turns undressing each other, exploring as they went, learning what it felt like to shed more than just their clothes. Each caress brought commitment, exposing the delicate layers of their hearts.

They touched each other intimately, but it wasn't foreplay, she thought. It was a vow—a need to give and take, make each other whole.

He kissed her bare belly, then slid lower to taste her with his tongue. She lifted her hips and moved against his mouth, inviting the climax that washed over her, the honeyed warmth traveling through her veins.

When the last wave subsided, Dakota smiled, a boyish grin rife with masculine satisfaction—a man content to give pleasure. Returning the favor, Annie knelt to lick his navel. His expression, that cowboy smile, turned instantly to need. She gave him the same unselfish pleasure, urging him toward their joining.

Gloriously naked, he rose above her, his gaze set deeply on hers. There would be no protection this time. Annie knew Dakota was offering more than himself. If their loving made a baby, then they would share another child—a son or daughter to complete their family.

He entered her, and together they found a wondrous rhythm.

Annie fell deeper in love with each stroke. Dakota Graywolf was her husband, the father of her adoptive children, a man who had been a part of her life since her own troubled youth.

She slid her hands over his skin, caressing the planes and angles that shaped his face, the well-toned muscles that formed his body. His stomach rippled, his heart pounded beneath her fingers. Such masculine beauty, she thought, as her orgasm ebbed and swelled, triggering his. Dakota kissed her when it happened, then flung back his head, his seed spilling warmth and promise.

He collapsed in her arms afterward, his breathing labored. Annie held him close, as close as possible. Tomorrow Dakota Graywolf would become a professional cowboy once again—a cowboy facing the biggest challenge of his life. A challenge that still frightened her.

She whispered a quiet prayer and combed her fingers through his hair. At least for tonight she could keep him safe in the circle of her arms.

Annie looked up from her room-service breakfast. Dakota stood before her in all his Western glory. Reminiscent of the famous cowboys who preceded him, his vintage turquoise shirt bore whipcord trim, silver conchos and an embroidered collar. Bat-wing chaps sported edges of long, turquoise fringe. A wide-brimmed Stetson rested on his head, and on his feet he wore shiny black boots.

Outlaw had booked him for an early-morning publicity appearance. He would be leaving shortly.

Annie glanced down at her plate. She had accepted the breakfast Dakota had ordered for her but couldn't bring herself to eat it. All she could think about was him riding that bull. Once he left, she wouldn't see him until the rodeo.

He tipped the hat with a flirtatious wink. "Come on, squirt, give me a smile."

A smile wasn't possible. Not now. "I'm still afraid, Dakota. And I'm worried that you are, too." His cowboy getup was part of an act, she thought. Striking as it was, it was just showbiz flash. Inside was a man preparing to ride the bull that had paralyzed him.

He removed his hat and knelt at her chair, urging her to meet his gaze. "I'm not scared anymore, and I'll tell you why. When the rodeo is over, I'm going to marry you again. Only this time with our children there and Harold and my parents, too. We're going to say our vows for everyone to hear, and we're going to mean them. This won't be a marriage of convenience anymore. This is for real, Annie."

She caressed his cheek, that warm sun-bronzed skin. The man she loved had just proposed, offered her a new beginning. "Then I'm going to put a ring on your finger." A white-gold band with a row of diamonds. She wanted the world to know that he was married, that this flashy cowboy belonged to her.

She would be his wife in every way, the woman who supported his dreams, eased his fears, held him at night. He wasn't her dad. Comparing them had been wrong. Dakota Graywolf was his own man—a dedicated husband and father—a man who had done his best to make her and the boys happy.

He took both of her hands in his. "Tell me you're not afraid anymore. Tell me you understand."

"I do." She understood that he had just given them both another reason to conquer the day. They had a wedding to plan, a future to live, children to raise. "You have to come back to me now. And you're going to be all right."

He skimmed her cheek. "Of course I am. Last time I didn't have you keeping me safe. Love is powerful medicine, Annie. We have to believe in it."

Yes, she thought. They had to believe in the power of love, had to believe in each other.

As he released her hands, their fingers slipped apart, but she knew an invisible current connected them still.

Hours later Annie sat beside her family at the rodeo, surrounded by familiar sights and sounds. Concession-stand popcorn blended with the aroma of hot dogs, nachos and livestock while a sea of Stetsons and a rain of Resistols shaded the stands like multi-hued umbrellas. In the arena, a bull blew out of the chute, a persistent cowboy on its back.

"I'm so glad you're here," Mary said.

Annie smiled at Dakota's sister while balancing a squirming Jamie on her lap. "Me, too."

The other woman pinched Jamie's cheek, making the boy laugh. "I'm glad my parents and Harold made it, also. It's too bad they're on the other side of the arena, though. I can't believe there was a ticket mix-up."

"We can meet up with them afterward." All of Dakota's family was there, Annie thought, offering their love and support. And that's what mattered most.

"So," Mary said, leaning in close, "from the look on your face, I'd be correct in assuming you and my brother worked out your differences."

"We did more than that," she whispered. "Dakota wants me to marry him again. This week, in fact, while we're all together."

"That will certainly please Harold. He'd probably love to give the bride away. I think he's been playing matchmaker all along."

"Really?"

Mary grinned, tossing her braid behind her. "Sure. With age comes wisdom, remember? But then again, Jill and I used to say that you and Dakota ought to get together. I'm sure she's smiling down on us right now."

Annie glanced up at the covered arena roof and imagined Jill's crooked smile. Miles had one just like it.

As though sensing his name in her thoughts, Miles peeked over. "See the rodeo clowns, Annie-Mom?" She nodded, and he continued, "They're called bullfighters. I heard the man say so."

She assumed "the man" was the disembodied voice of the announcer. "Are you enjoying the rodeo?" she asked her son.

"Yeah. Me and Tye know all about bull riding. You gotta bend your arm like this." He raised his arm, mimicking the cowboy in the arena. "And you gotta hold on to the rope with your other hand."

Annie gazed out at the bull rider as he landed on the ground and scrambled to his feet. She knew it wasn't quite that simple. She closed her eyes and said a quiet prayer for her dad. He was a reckless man, but in his own way he had loved her.

Jamie crawled back to his seat and bounced between his brothers. Tyler handed the boy a popcorn carton and smiled at Annie. She knew how happy Tyler was to see her there.

The commentator continued to talk, highlighting each cowboy's background and announcing scores. As Annie watched, anxiety mounted. Dakota would be riding soon.

After the bull riding competition ended, the announcer teased the crowd, asking if they were ready for more. A thunder of cheers and whistles made up the collective response. Annie scooted to the edge of her seat.

"I'm sure Excalibur's ready," the announcer said. "That bull's always ready for a fight. But then again, so is Dakota Graywolf."

At the mention of Dakota's name, another wall of whoops and hollers thundered through the arena. Annie listened while the commentator went into a short bio of Dakota's rodeo history and then dramatically rehashed his last bout with Excalibur. "But this veteran cowboy's back on his feet and determined to make rodeo history," he said. "And I just got word it's about to happen."

Along with Annie thousands of spectators leaned forward. "It's Daddy's turn to ride," Tyler told Jamie, taking the child's hand.

Excalibur blasted out of the chute in a cloud of dust, turned and spun, rocking and jarring Dakota. The bull moved at an angry pace, bucking and spinning. Annie thought Dakota's long, fluid body made the jerking ride look almost poetic. The edges of his chaps rose, flapping the turquoise fringe.

The announcer talked, but Annie didn't listen. She focused all of her senses on her husband, on his beauty and power. She smiled and touched the tips of her fingers together, instantly feeling Dakota's energy. *I'm inside of him,* she thought. *I'm a part of his spirit. He knows I'm here.*

The buzz of the eight-second whistle broke her concentration, the commentator's voice returning to her ears. "He did it, ladies and gentlemen. Dakota Graywolf rode the unrideable bull. And what a ride…"

The audience whooped and howled, whistled and applauded, but a moment later, as Dakota attempted to dismount the bucking bull, the cheers turned to gasps. Dakota was hung up, his hand caught beneath the rope secured to the bull.

Annie's heart stopped. While his feet dragged and his body slapped against Excalibur's, the bullfighters dashed to his aid. Although they made frenzied attempts to free him, it was to no avail. Dakota remained trapped, struggling to dodge Excalibur's furious turns and kicks. His hat flew off and was immediately crushed beneath the animal's pounding hoofs.

Jamie cried, "Daddy!" and scrambled for his mother.

"Oh, please, not again, not again," Mary chanted as Jamie tumbled across her lap and into Annie's trembling arms.

It's not happening again, Annie thought. Dakota hadn't been hung up last time. He'd been bucked off, and when he'd hit the ground, Excalibur, still in a kicking rage, had spun around and stepped on him. This time Dakota had a chance.

"Oh, Lord." A male spectator behind Annie worried, his frantic words bordering on a prayer. "If he gets trapped under that bull…"

"He won't," Annie said, loud enough for her family to hear. "He's going to be fine."

Love is a powerful medicine. We have to believe in it.

Within a heartbeat Dakota fell free and landed against one of the bullfighters. They both hit the ground and rolled to their feet. Excalibur was herded back to the pen in a storm of dust.

Dakota staggered, located his mangled hat, then bowed to the crowd.

Applause thundered as the audience rocked the stands in a rousing ovation.

Tears filled Annie's eyes. Dakota stood in the center of the arena, a little disoriented, but smiling. He scanned the crowd as though trying to regain his sense of direction. A moment later he headed toward the section where she and the kids sat, looking more gorgeous than ever, his hair mussed, boots dusty, turquoise fringe rustling.

The announcer followed his moves, speaking all the while. "This veteran bull rider's one happy cowboy. Limping a little more than usual, and most likely bruised, but doing just fine." The voice paused as the crowd waited and watched, all eyes on Dakota.

Annie leaned forward. All eyes were on her, too. The champion bull rider was making his way toward her, over the rail that divided them and into her willing arms.

She kissed him while the audience cheered again, the people near them enjoying a private show. Annie dried her eyes as Dakota turned toward his sons. He reached for Jamie and lifted the boy. Annie could see the effort it took, realizing her husband was ignoring his own discomfort, determined to erase the two-year-old's worried frown.

"Daddy okay?" the child asked, studying his father. "You no hurt?"

"I'm doing great, sport," he answered, winking at Tyler and Miles, then grinning at Mary. "I've never been better."

Mary kissed his cheek. "That was some show. You gave us quite a scare."

"Annie kept me safe," he whispered, drawing her and the children into a family hug. "Loving her is my medicine."

Yes, Annie thought, admiring the dusty cowboy at her side. The Otter and the Lynx had found each other at last, and love was their medicine. The answer to their future. The unconditional bond that would keep them together forever.

They went back to the same chapel, but Annie wore a different dress and Dakota a different suit, new clothes for the start of their new life.

The Reverend Matthews displayed a brighter smile this time, and his wife played the organ with even more gusto. Dakota was a celebrity in their eyes. Almost all of Las Vegas had heard about him by now—the cowboy who had challenged Excalibur and won.

Jamie carried the ring Annie had purchased for Dakota,

dropping it on his way to the front of the chapel, then retrieving it with stubby brown fingers and a youthful grin.

Mary stood at the altar and encouraged Jamie's trek with an outstretched hand. The boy took the offering and waved to his father, who waited patiently for his bride, his bruised ribs wrapped carefully beneath a crisp shirt.

Harold walked Annie down the carpeted aisle. He was a small man, not much taller than she, but he carried himself with strength and pride. When he presented Annie to her groom, he smiled, the lines around his eyes crinkling in delight. His copper skin was filled with a lifetime of memories, a wrinkle for each year of his existence—much like an ancient tree boasting its age.

Tyler and Miles sat with Tucker and Katherine Graywolf, the parents Annie had come to love as her own. Tucker looked like an older version of Dakota, an indication of how wonderfully her husband would age. His jet-black hair bore subtle streaks of gray, his shoulders wide, his jaw still taut. Katherine, tall and lovely in an exquisite floral dress, wore a silver pendant Dakota had made. She doted on the boys, easily accepting her role as their Cheyenne grandmother.

Annie's mind drifted back to the first time she had met Dakota. His ribs were bruised then, too. He had been long and lean, a teenage boy with messy hair and a charming smile—a young cowboy who had fallen from a bull and dusted himself off, ignoring the injury he'd sustained the day before. Annie had watched him through adoring eyes, instantly wanting to fix his hurt.

But it was he who had fixed hers instead, she decided. He had taught her the meaning of love and acceptance.

She placed the white-gold band on his finger and smiled. Tonight they would share a honeymoon suite as Annie and Dakota Graywolf.

Newlyweds. Lovers. Husband and wife.

Epilogue

Home, Dakota thought. He was home. And not just in body, but in spirit.

He smiled at his wife as she unpacked their lunch. They had saddled the horses and ridden to a secluded spot, the area lush and green, thriving with life. He turned toward the boys. This was a family outing, a picnic rife with sunshine and all the wonderful chaos that came with being a parent. A pet owner, too. Dog Soldier had trailed behind them, intent on joining the festivities. The mixed-breed, it appeared, had appointed himself the family guardian, patrolling the picnic area in the same nonintrusive manner in which he patrolled their backyard.

Jamie caught Dakota's eye, and he noticed a pout on the child's face. "What's wrong, sport?"

"Why we not bring J-miah?"

He took the two-year-old into his arms. It felt so natural to hold his son and rest his chin on the top of the boy's head. "Jeremiah likes to stay home. He's the kind of dog who enjoys sleeping all day." He chuckled to himself, imagining the bulldog huffing and puffing to keep up. No, Jeremiah wasn't exactly the athletic type.

"How come Taco here?"

Dakota cuddled Jamie a little closer. "He's not. We all agreed Taco was too little to come along."

"But him here," the child protested.

Dakota raised an eyebrow and looked across the blanket at Miles. Sure enough, Taco peeked out from the five-year-old's backpack. Dakota bit the inside of his cheek to keep from laughing. The Chihuahua cocked its head, looking more like an overgrown mouse than a dog, its ears bent at a comical angle.

He didn't have the heart to reprimand Miles, yet this didn't seem fair to Jamie. "We'll have a special picnic just for Jeremiah," he told his youngest son. "Tomorrow, in the backyard, okay?"

Jamie nodded vigorously and wiggled out of Dakota's arms, anxious to interrupt the checkers game his older brothers played. Tyler took the little boy's hand as he approached, welcoming him with affection. A lump formed in Dakota's throat. Tyler—sweet, sensitive Tyler—the protective big brother.

While the boys played their game, Annie moved closer to Dakota, then slipped her arms around his neck.

"You're a terrific father," she said.

He turned his head to nuzzle her cheek. "I like being a dad." It felt right to have a wife and kids. His Cheyenne commitment still applied, but love had been tossed into the mix. Dakota loved his family—loved them beyond comprehension.

"How would you feel about having a daughter?" Annie asked, her mouth still pressed against his ear.

His heartbeat quickened. He took her hands and faced her, studying those whisky eyes. "Are you? Are we?"

"It's too soon to tell, but I think so." She slipped her fingers through his, warming him with her touch. "For months I've been seeing this baby girl in my head, sort of like a vision, I guess. But last night I dreamed about her, and she seemed so real."

Because she was, Dakota realized. A baby grew in Annie's

womb—a daughter. He didn't need a scientific test to tell him
what Annie's dream meant. The answer was already there,
shining in his wife's eyes.

As a gentle breeze stirred the leaves on the trees, Dakota
knew it was a message from Maheo, the Creator of life. Yes,
a child nestled in Annie's womb, a baby conceived in love.

Dakota placed his head against Annie's tummy and smiled.
The Cheyenne dad was right where he belonged—with his
family—honoring his wife and children. The greatest blessing
a man could have.

*   *   *   *   *

*Talented author Sheri WhiteFeather
will delight romance readers with
another of her ultraemotional
Native American love stories,*

NIGHT WIND'S WOMAN,

*available in November 2000
from Silhouette Desire.*

Multi-*New York Times* bestselling author

NORA ROBERTS

knew from the first how to capture readers' hearts.
Celebrate the 20th Anniversary of Silhouette Books
with this special 2-in-1 edition containing her fabulous
first book and the sensational sequel.

Coming in June

IRISH HEARTS

Adelia Cunnane's fiery temper sets proud, powerful horse
breeder Travis Grant's heart aflame and he resolves to
make this wild *Irish Thoroughbred* his own.

Erin McKinnon accepts wealthy Burke Logan's loveless
proposal, but can this ravishing *Irish Rose* win her
hard-hearted husband's love?

Also available in June from
Silhouette Special Edition (SSE #1328)

IRISH REBEL

In this brand-new sequel to *Irish Thoroughbred*, Travis and
Adelia's innocent but strong-willed daughter Keeley discovers
love in the arms of a charming Irish rogue with a talent for
horses...and romance.

Where love comes alive™

ENTER FOR
A CHANCE TO WIN*

Silhouette's 20ᵗʰ Anniversary Contest

Tell Us Where in the World
You Would Like *Your* Love To Come Alive...
And We'll Send the Lucky Winner There!

Silhouette wants to take you wherever
your happy ending can come true.

Here's how to enter: Tell us, in 100 words or less,
where you want to go to make your love come alive!

In addition to the grand prize, there will be 200
runner-up prizes, collector's-edition book sets
autographed by one of the Silhouette anniversary
authors: **Nora Roberts**, **Diana Palmer**,
Linda Howard or **Annette Broadrick**.

DON'T MISS YOUR CHANCE TO WIN!
ENTER NOW! No Purchase Necessary

Silhouette®
Where love comes alive™

Visit Silhouette at www.eHarlequin.com to enter, starting this summer.

Name: _____

Address: _____

City: _____ State/Province: _____

Zip/Postal Code: _____

Mail to Harlequin Books: **In the U.S.**: P.O. Box 9069, Buffalo, NY
14269-9069; **In Canada**: P.O. Box 637, Fort Erie, Ontario, L4A 5X3